"Did you think I was seeing a mistress?"

Bart's voice was mocking as he asked the question.

"Well, you said you had one!" Eve was beginning to realize that if she weren't careful Bart would discover that she was jealous. "The first night we met you said—"

"I believe I said a lot of things that night," he recalled harshly. "But then you were at your most provocative!"

"Does that mean you don't have a mistress?"

"What's the matter, Miss Icicle Heart? Don't you like other people to enjoy themselves?" he taunted.

"You can do whatever you please," she told him heatedly. Loving this man didn't make him any less an arrogant tease. "And I don't have an icicle heart."

"Then maybe you don't have a heart at all," he dismissed her scathingly.

CAROLE MORTIMER
is also the author of these

Harlequin Presents

Many of these titles are available at your local bookseller.

For a free catalogue listing all available Harlequin Romances
and Harlequin Presents, send your name and address to:

HARLEQUIN READER SERVICE
1440 South Priest Drive, Tempe, AZ 85281
Canadian address: Stratford, Ontario N5A 6W2

CAROLE MORTIMER

red rose for love

Harlequin Books

TORONTO • LONDON • LOS ANGELES • AMSTERDAM
SYDNEY • HAMBURG • PARIS • STOCKHOLM • ATHENS • TOKYO

For
John and Matthew

———————————•———————————

Harlequin Presents first edition August 1982
ISBN 0-373-10522-3

Original hardcover edition published in 1982
by Mills & Boon Limited

CHAPTER ONE

SHE had been good, her performance perfect. She knew it and so did the audience; their wild applause brought an excited flush to Eve's animated features. The applause was deafening, and they wouldn't allow her to leave the stage.

Finally Eve had to give them one more song, silence falling over the standing people as she once again took up the microphone, waiting for everyone to be seated again before she indicated to her backing musicians to start playing.

It was her latest song, the song she had begun the concert with, and the audience loved it now as they had then. This time she didn't wait for the cries for more, but took a hasty bow and left the stage, exhausted by the last two hours of her one-woman concert.

Her long dark hair was clinging damply to her forehead, falling smoothly over her shoulder, its straightness gleaming jet-black. She brushed the damp tendrils from her face, her hands long and slender, her nails long and lacquered the same purple of the clinging catsuit she wore.

She looked to neither left nor right as she made her way to her dressing-room, a bright meaningless smile on her lips as the congratulations came her way from the staff who worked just as hard behind the scenes as she did before the audience.

Derek James, her manager, was waiting for her when she entered her dressing-room. 'Great concert, Eve,' he said excitedly. 'You're really made now. Everyone will be queueing up to book you.'

Eve sat down before the mirror, anxious to remove the heavy make-up she had worn on stage, wanting to cream her naturally peachy skin before wiping her face clean. She took out her bottle of lotion.

'Don't do that yet,' Derek stopped her. 'You look about sixteen without your make-up. Wait until we get away from here. There'll probably be some fans waiting outside.'

'You know I hate this look.' She grimaced at her reflection, the face make-up giving her skin a dark glow, the eye make-up several shades of purple, her naturally dark lashes thickened by the dark mascara she had applied, her lips darkened by the plum-coloured lipstick. She looked totally unlike herself, and she hated it.

'You may not like it,' Derek put the lotion back in the drawer unused, 'but the public loves it—and they're the ones that count.'

'Yes,' she sighed, brushing her long hair free of tangles.

'Don't knock it.' He pulled up a chair and sat down, straddling it, his arms resting on the back. 'You were tremendous tonight, Eve. I've never seen you so—so damned sexy!' he said with enthusiasm. 'What happened to you out there?'

She shrugged. 'I gave them what they wanted.'

'And it worked! God, how it worked. You'll be booked up for work for years to come.'

Her mouth twisted. 'I can see the pound notes registering in your eyes. If I make money then so do you,' she derided.

'Talking of money,' he took no offence at her rebuke, 'you had a rich fan out there tonight.'

Eve instantly stiffened, her hand trembling slightly as she reapplied her lipstick. 'Oh?' She forced indifference into her voice.

'Yes. Bartholomew Jordan. You've heard of him, haven't you?' Derek asked anxiously.

'Who hasn't?' she said lightly, her tension leaving her. It wasn't Carl! After all, not every rich man could be him. Besides, there was absolutely no reason to suppose he would ever come to hear her sing again.

Derek looked disappointed by her lack of enthusiasm. A man of thirty, with an untidy attractiveness, he always looked as if he had just crawled out of bed, his clothes always badly creased, his hair untidy. He and Eve had met almost five years ago, when she was twenty and being badly managed by a man who had no interest in the style of music she projected. Derek had taken over her career from that moment, until she had now reached the peak of giving her own concert to a full audience, an audience fully attuned to her style of music, to the hard-rock songs and contrasting love songs that she enjoyed singing.

'I said Bartholomew Jordan, Eve,' Derek repeated crossly. '*The* Bartholomew Jordan.'

She nodded. 'The banker.'

'And the rest. The man's a billionaire.'

'Then what's he doing at *my* concert?' she dismissed scathingly, and stood up, a tall girl made even taller by the high-heeled sandals she wore. 'I'm exhausted, Derek,' she told him wearily. 'I want to go home. And sleep, and sleep, and sleep,' she yawned tiredly.

Derek shook his head. 'You can't do that. Mr Jordan wants to meet you.'

She pulled a face. 'Then he'll have to want. I'm too tired, Derek,' she insisted as he went to protest. 'I'm not in the mood to pamper an old man, even if he is rich as Croesus.'

'Jordan isn't old——'

'Not unless you call thirty-nine old,' drawled a third person.

Eve turned slowly, her expression giving nothing away as she looked at the man now standing in the open doorway. Yes, this would be Bartholomew Jordan; he just oozed confidence in himself and his power over other people. He was impressive to look at in the dark pin-striped suit, white silk shirt, and meticulously tied tie, his blond good looks a startling contrast to his deep tan. His hair was several shades of blond, from white to pure gold, in an overlong wind-swept style, his deep green eyes watching her mock-ingly, his lashes long and dark, his nose straight, his firm mouth curved into a questioning smile, his jaw strong and purposeful.

Yes, he was impressive—and Eve wasn't impressed at all. She raised her eyebrows, controlled under that insolent stare. 'They say eavesdroppers never hear anything good about themselves,' she told him in her naturally husky tone.

Derek gave her a frowning look. 'Eve——'

'Would you leave Miss Meredith and me to talk?' Bartholomew Jordan walked farther into the room, holding the door open for Derek to leave.

Eve faced him unflinchingly. 'I believe you heard me say I was tired, Mr Jordan.' She picked up her handbag and swished out of the room, down the corridor and out of the stage-door without a second glance.

She was instantly surrounded by enthusiastic fans, signing one or two autographs before she realised she was going to have difficulty getting away from here. She was being pushed and jostled, hands coming out just to touch her. She cringed from those hands.

Suddenly her elbow was taken in a firm grasp, and she was propelled firmly out of the crowd towards a waiting car. 'Thanks, Der—You!' she gasped as she looked straight into the deep green eyes of Bartholomew Jordan. She tried to pull out of his grasp.

'Would you please let me go,' she ordered coldly.

'Gladly,' he drawled. 'If you want me to leave you to the mercy of that mob,' he nodded behind her.

Eve followed his line of vision. If anything the crowd had increased in number. 'No,' she sighed, 'I don't want you to do that.'

'Then get inside,' he commanded curtly.

The chauffeur had appeared at the back of the car and was even now opening the door for them. Eve got in, moving over as far as she could as Bartholomew Jordan climbed in beside her, the door firmly closed before the chauffeur got in behind the wheel. The window between the driver and the back of the car was firmly closed, leaving the two of them in complete privacy.

Eve was aware of the smell of expensive cologne, a tangy elusive smell that in no way detracted from this man's own animal smell. She could also detect the aroma of cigars or cheroots, this smell as pleasant as the cologne.

'Just how did you intend getting home this evening?' he asked in that pleasant well-modulated voice that spoke of an expensive education.

She shrugged dismissively. 'I was going to ask Derek to call me a taxi.'

His mouth twisted derisively. 'After the performance you gave this evening you're lucky to get away in one piece.'

'I'm sorry I displeased you——'

'You didn't,' he cut in on her sarcasm. 'The opposite.'

Her head went back, her long dark hair gleaming down her back. 'I hardly expected to make such an impression.'

His green-eyed gaze ran appraisingly over her clearly defined curves in the shimmering body-hugging material of her cat-suit. 'In that outfit you don't even need to sing to make an impression.'

Eve flushed at the familiarity in his voice. 'Mr Jordan——'

'Bart,' he put in softly.

She blinked up at him, her eyes very blue. 'Bart?'

He nodded, his hair very blond. 'All my friends call me Bart.' He took a cheroot out of the case in his breast-pocket. 'Do you mind?' he asked politely.

'Not at all. And I'm not a friend, Mr Jordan,' she told him coldly. 'And I have no intention of ever becoming one.' The smell of his cheroot filled the car as he returned his gold lighter to his pocket, using the expensive item as if it meant nothing to him.

'Never?' he quirked an eyebrow.

'Most of *my* friends are of years' standing,' she said coolly. 'Now could you please drop me off here? I can easily get a taxi now.'

'Let me drive you to your home.'

'I don't live in London.'

'Then I'll drive you to wherever it is you want to go,' he offered smoothly.

Eve controlled her anger with effort. This man liked his own way, that much was obvious, but men like him left her cold. Over-confident, arrogant, and high-handed—Bartholomew Jordan fitted that description as if it had been made for him.

'I *want* to go here, Mr Jordan,' she sat forward, 'if you could ask your driver to stop.'

'Why?' came his stark query.

Her eyes flashed deeply blue. 'Maybe because I like to choose my own company.'

His eyes narrowed, his expression thoughtful. 'You don't like me. Why?'

'Like I said, I like to choose my own company.'

'And given that choice?'

'I certainly wouldn't choose you!' she said rudely.

'Derek James?'

She looked startled. 'I beg your pardon?'

His expression was haughty. 'He informed me you were spending the night at his apartment.'

And so she was, but in a separate bedroom! Not that this man would believe that, he wouldn't understand such a sterile relationship. He was everything she most despised, over-confident, and over-wealthy, believing that wealth could buy him anything he wanted. And right now he probably thought it could buy him a place in her bed!

She gave him a derisive look. 'I am. I always stay with Derek when I'm in town.' She didn't explain to him that she also stayed with Derek's wife, Judy.

Bartholomew Jordan's mouth twisted. 'What a nice arrangement!'

She shrugged. 'We like it.'

He studied the glowing tip of his cheroot. 'No chance of your dropping him?'

Her eyes widened. 'Are you propositioning me?' she asked slowly, disbelievingly.

He smiled a humourless smile. 'I'm sure it isn't the first time.'

Eve licked her dry lips, anger boiling up within her. 'What are you offering?' Her voice was controlled, too controlled if he did but know it.

He frowned. 'What do you want?'

'What does the woman in your life now get?'

He stiffened, searching her emotionless features with narrowed eyes. 'What makes you think there is a woman?'

'Nothing about you makes me think there isn't,' she scorned. 'So, what's the asking price?'

'An apartment, financial security, jewels?' he said tautly.

'All of them?'

'If you like,' he nodded abruptly.

She seemed to consider. 'And your time?'

He frowned his puzzlement. 'My time?'

Eve nodded. 'How often could I expect you to visit me?'

His frown deepened, his eyes glacial. 'As often as I could,' he said slowly.

'Which would be?' she persisted.

'Once or twice a week.'

'Oh, that wouldn't suit me at all,' Eve dismissed, bending forward to press the button that lowered the dividing window. 'Could you stop here?' she requested the driver.

'Mr Jordan?' he said uncertainly.

'Drive on, Adam,' Bartholomew Jordan instructed, closing the window again. 'That wasn't very clever, Eve.' His voice had hardened to anger.

She turned. 'I wasn't trying to be clever,' she told him coldly. 'I've been working for weeks to get this concert together, this last week has been hell, tonight was exhausting, and now I have to sit here and take insults from you! You can take your proposition, Mr Jordan, and——'

'I think what you're going to say next isn't ladylike,' he cut in firmly.

'Maybe it wasn't,' she rasped, 'but it was a damn sight more honest than what you've been saying to me. Why don't you just tell me you want to go to bed with me and be done with it!'

He drew in an angry breath. 'All right,' he nodded, 'I do want to go to bed with you. Now. Tonight.' He stubbed out the half-smoked cheroot.

'Go to hell!' she spat the words at him.

'What is it about the arrangement you don't like? Ah yes,' he drawled, 'the amount of time I would spend with you. Was it too much or too little?'

'Too much!' she snapped. 'Even sitting in this car with you now is too much. Men like you sicken me, Mr Jordan. You——' She didn't get any further; his mouth was savage on hers.

She didn't give him the satisfaction of fighting him, but lay placid in his arms as he kissed her with complete thoroughness. He left her cold, as she had known he would; his seduction was practised, his kisses designed to extract a response even from the most reluctant of females. Although she doubted he ever met ones that were reluctant.

But *she* was, her eyes spitting venom at him when he at last raised his head. A dark flush coloured his cheeks, his eyes narrowed angrily, his fingers biting into the soft flesh of her arms.

'What did that prove, Mr Jordan?' she scorned, shaking off his hands and straightening her tousled hair.

He sat back, that deep flush the only sign that he was at all put out by her lack of response. 'It proved,' he said slowly, 'that your stage act is just that—an act.'

Eve gave him a startled look. 'What do you mean?'

'On stage you look incredibly sexy——'

'And I don't now?' she taunted, knowing very well that she did.

He obviously knew it too. 'I didn't say that. There's just no back-up to that act you put on for the audience.'

Her mouth twisted. 'Because I'm not falling over myself with gratitude that you want me?' she scorned. 'Because I find your offer insulting in the extreme? Because I didn't collapse in ecstasy when you kissed me? Well, I'm sorry, Mr Jordan, but as you said, it's far from the first time I've been propositioned. And far from the first time I've said no!'

His eyes were cold now, like chips of green glass. 'I should think the matter over seriously before you do that.'

Eve became still. 'Are you threatening me?'

He raised his eyebrows. 'Did it sound as if I were?'

'Yes!' she hissed.

He shrugged. 'Then I suppose I must have been.'

Eve drew in an angry breath, sitting forward to once again press the button to lower the dividing window. 'Stop this car immediately,' she ordered the driver. 'Don't ask your employer's permission,' she said tautly. 'Just do it!'

'Sir?' he requested hesitantly.

'Do it, Adam,' Bartholomew Jordan drawled. 'When it's convenient to do so.'

Eve didn't look at Bartholomew Jordan again. As soon as the limousine came to a halt beside the pavement she rushed to get out, only to find Adam there before her, his expression blank as he held the door open for her. Maybe it wasn't the first time his employer had been turned down, after all.

'Thank you,' she told the chauffeur huskily, stepping back as he closed the door, hailing a taxi as she saw one driving slowly down the street towards her, its 'For Hire' sign alight.

Amazingly it stopped behind the still parked limousine, and Eve climbed gratefully inside, relaxing back in the seat once she had given the driver Derek's address, not looking at the limousine as they pulled out in front of it.

She wasn't lying when she told Bartholomew Jordan that she had been propositioned many times before. In her profession she was bound to be, but never ever as arrogantly as he had done. And no one had ever gone to the extreme of making threats before either!

She became aware of the taxi-driver shooting her

questioning looks in the driving-mirror. 'Is there anything wrong?' she frowned.

'Er—no, love. I—I was just wondering,' he spoke in
a broad Cockney accent, 'are you Eve Meredith, the
singer?'

She flushed, her embarrassment acute at being
recognised in this way. 'I am,' she admitted softly.

'I thought so,' he grinned at her in the mirror. 'My
daughter's a fan of yours. She went to your concert
tonight.' He chuckled. 'Just wait until I tell her I
actually drove you home!'

'Not home,' Eve hastily corrected that impression,
not wanting people she didn't know suddenly appearing on the doorstep. 'Just to a friend's.'

'I picked up Cliff Richard last week,' he told her. 'A
real gentleman, he is.'

She could imagine he was, the ever-youthful superstar seemed to be liked by most people.

They were fast approaching Derek's apartment now,
and she once again felt the exhaustion wash over her.
Tomorrow she would have to go back to the theatre
and do the whole show over again, and right now she
badly wanted to sleep and regenerate her weary body.

'No charge,' the driver told her once they were
parked. 'It's been a real pleasure to drive you. Not
very often I get to meet a celebrity.'

She wouldn't exactly put herself in that class, but
she accepted his generosity in the mood it was given. It
was only as she stepped out on to the pavement that
she noticed the dark limousine behind them, a limousine that swooshed smoothly past them, turning
right at the end of the road, Bartholomew Jordan's
limousine!

The damned man had followed her to Derek's home!
Oh, that man was past enduring! She wouldn't be
harassed in this way, especially by a man like him. Any

more trouble from him and she would call in the police. She doubted he would like that.

Derek wasn't yet home when she let herself into the apartment, but his wife Judy was. She rose out of an armchair at Eve's entrance, a small girl with frizzed blonde hair and a gaminely attractive face.

'Wonderful concert, Eve,' she hugged her.

'Thanks.' Eve gave a wan smile. 'No Derek?' There was always the possibility he could be in the bedroom.

'He stayed behind to finish things up there.'

Eve at once felt guilty. 'I should have done that,' she sighed, collapsing into a chair and closing her eyes. 'God, I'm tired!'

'Go to bed,' Judy encouraged. 'There's no reason for you to wait up for Derek.'

Eve opened her eyes, new life flooding into her weary body. 'Oh yes, there is,' she said firmly.

Judy raised her eyebrows. 'That sounds ominous.'

'It is.' After all, it was Derek's fault that she had met Bartholomew Jordan.

'Oh dear!'

Eve forced a smile to her stiff lips. 'Don't worry, I just have a few questions to ask him.' Like how forcefully Bartholomew Jordan had said he wanted to meet her!

'I'll make some coffee,' Judy offered. 'It will help to keep us awake.'

It did, just. And when Derek arrived home forty minutes later Eve woke up completely.

'How did you get on with Jordan?' was his first query.

She frowned. 'You saw how I got on with him,' she said guardedly.

He sat down beside her. 'I meant later.' He didn't seem to notice her darkening expression. 'Boy, he followed you like the devil himself!'

'I think he is the devil himself,' Eve said with disgust.

Derek looked disappointed. 'You didn't like him.'

'Did you expect me to?' she challenged.

He pulled a face. 'I hoped you would.'

'Well, I didn't!' she told him vehemently, her usually calm features animated with her dislike of the man.

'Pity.' Derek looked away, standing up to pace the room, a worried frown to his face.

Eve tensed. 'How much of a pity?' she asked slowly.

His expression became evasive. 'He's a powerful man,' he shrugged. 'It never pays to antagonise men like that.'

Judy looked puzzled. 'Are we talking about *Bart* Jordan?'

'Judy——'

'Yes,' Eve cut across Derek's warning. 'Yes, we're talking about Bart Jordan, Judy. What do you know about him?'

The other girl frowned. 'Well, I—I—Derek?' she looked at him appealingly.

'Okay,' Eve sighed, 'Derek can tell me. What about Bart Jordan, Derek?'

He shrugged. 'I already told you, he isn't a good man to make an enemy of. Make us some coffee, sweetheart?' he requested of his wife.

Eve knew it was a way of getting the other girl out of the room, which only heightened her suspicions. 'Derek!' she said firmly once they were alone. 'I want to know what's going on.'

He threw himself back down into the armchair, one leg hanging over the arm. 'Nothing is going on,' he dismissed tersely, a sure sign that he was agitated. He was usually so even-tempered that Eve knew there was something wrong.

She frowned, biting her bottom lip. 'Why do I get

the feeling there's something you aren't telling me?'

'I have no idea,' he dismissed. 'Shouldn't you be getting to bed? You have a long day ahead of you to-morrow.'

'And the day after that, and the day after that,' she grimaced. 'A week of this and I'll be dead.'

'A week of this and you'll be made,' Derek corrected.

She quirked an eyebrow. 'I thought I already was,' she reminded him, tongue-in-cheek.

'Yeah, well—wait until you see the reviews in the morning!' His enthusiasm was never dampened for long, in fact it was this enthusiasm that had got Eve this far.

She stood up. 'Don't wake me,' she instructed tiredly.

'Not even for the reviews?'

'Not even for them,' she groaned, aching in every bone of her body. Her stage show involved dancing as well as singing.

'Rehearsals at eleven sharp,' he reminded her, his mind firmly on business as usual.

'Don't remind me!' She staggered into her bed-room.

Without Derek's prodding and hard work Eve doubted she would ever have risen above touring the seedy clubs she had been working in when they had first met. At the time she had been happy with her lot, had accepted what she felt to be her limitations, had lacked the drive and ambition to get even as far as she was today, let alone the superstar bracket Derek had mapped out for her. But Derek had pushed her on until now she had one hit record behind her, another new release, and now this concert.

Derek had worked so hard on her behalf, had begged and stolen work for her, until the last six months her career had really taken off. She couldn't exactly be called an overnight success, although the public recognition, such as the taxi-driver's, still came as something of a surprise to her.

Had Carl seen her success? Did he ever regret the way he had forced her out of his life?

Damn Carl! She hadn't thought of him for months—well, weeks—well, actually it was days, but who was counting? Bartholomew Jordan had brought back the memories of Carl, one more reason why she hated him. Just another rich man who thought his money could buy him everything, including love!

She could finally remove the detested make-up, and felt cleaner and fresher once that was done. She studied her reflection in the mirror. Derek was right, she did look about sixteen without the make-up; she also, to her mind, looked more attractive.

At the end of the week she could go back to Norfolk and be just the nonentity Eve Meredith, could go back to her houseboat and live a normal life again. Derek had promised her a holiday after this week of concerts, and she could hardly wait to get back to Norfolk. Maybe she wasn't really cut out for stardom, although this was a hell of a time to discover it, and Derek felt sure that she could make it right to the top. Still, much as she valued him as a friend, she still knew that fifteen per cent of nothing was nothing.

She turned over in the bed. Heavens, she was an ungrateful bitch tonight! Everything was sure to look brighter in the morning.

It did. She felt revitalised by her long sleep, her usual energy back in evidence. The reviews were good but guarded, speculating as to whether her dazzling performance could be maintained throughout the week.

'I'll show them!' she told Derek, throwing the newspapers down in disgust.

He smiled. 'That's my girl!'

Rehearsals went perfectly, any minor adjustments that needed to be made being quickly ironed out. After a couple of hours of this she was ready to go back to the apartment and rest. She was delicately made, very slender, and she would need all the energy she could muster for the gruelling evening ahead of her. Maybe the critics were right after all, maybe she didn't have the stamina for this sort of life.

When she arrived back at the flat it was to find the biggest bouquet of red roses she had ever seen in her life lying on the doorstep; both Judy and Derek were out. She recoiled just at the sight of them, her expression darkening as she read the card that went with them. It was signed simply 'Bart'.

The roses went straight into the dustbin, the card along with them. God, that man was really pushing his luck! Bart, indeed! Only his so-called 'friends' called him that!

She was so steamed up she must have paced the apartment for half an hour or more, sleep completely forgotten. She was so angry that she sent him a telegram in the end; it read, 'Received and discarded, *Eve Meredith*'. She sent it to his bank, knowing that something as important as a telegram would reach him wherever he was.

That would show him what she thought of him *and* his roses!

It was when she woke up that the uncertainty set in. Much as she disliked Bartholomew Jordan and everything he represented, he really wasn't a man she should antagonise. And the telegram had been a childish gesture. It should have been enough that *she* knew she had destroyed the roses. This way she was inviting retribution.

But it seemed not. A second bouquet of roses appeared at the theatre that evening, this time signed 'Bartholomew Jordan'. He had to have received her telegram by now. Unless he had placed the order for these roses before he had received it? But that didn't make sense, not when he had signed the second card so formally.

He certainly was a persistent man, surprisingly so, although it was doubtful that he needed to be this persistent normally; most women would be falling over themselves just to be associated with him.

Derek's eyebrows rose as he saw the roses still lying in their cellophane on the table where Eve had thrown them. 'An admirer?' he asked curiously, obviously looking for the card she had put away in her handbag.

'One with more money than sense,' she nodded. Her cat-suit was a deep red this evening, her hair long and crinkled from the tight plaits she had bound it in after washing it this afternoon. Her make-up was just as dramatic, her mouth a deep slash of red to match the suit.

'Here,' Derek broke off one of the roses and pushed it into her hair over her ear. It gave her the look of a wild gypsy. 'Perfect,' he nodded his approval.

Eve pulled the rose out of her hair, throwing it in the bin. 'It would wilt before the end of the performance,' she said stiffly as she saw Derek's shocked face.

'You could have replaced it during the break,' he said practically.

Her head went back. 'I'd rather not.'

He frowned. 'Who are they from?'

'Guess,' she invited dryly, hoping he would put her dislike of the deep red blooms down to their sender.

His face brightened. 'Not Bart Jordan?'

'All right,' she agreed. 'Not Bart Jordan.'

'Don't tease, Eve,' he said seriously.

She turned angrily to face him. 'What is it about this man? Why is he so special? I've had men like him interested in me before, but you never tried to tell me how to behave with them.'

He flushed. 'I'm not telling you how to behave with Jordan either. I just don't think it would do us any good for you to upset him. He has a lot of influence, he could make things very uncomfortable for us if he chose to.'

'And do you think he might?' She remembered the threat in Bartholomew Jordan's voice.

'I think he could do,' Derek nodded.

'And what do you suggest I do about it?' she asked tartly. 'Sleep with him just to make sure he stays sweet?'

Derek flushed. 'I didn't say that——'

'I'm so sorry,' her voice dripped sarcasm. 'Maybe it just sounded that way to me.'

He gave an impatient sigh. 'You're impossible in this mood, Eve. It wouldn't do you any harm to be nice to him.'

She stood up. 'He doesn't want me to be *nice* to him, he wants to go to bed with me!'

'I'll admit he's attracted to you, but——'

'He told me what he wants, Derek,' she interrupted firmly. 'He wants *me*, in his bed. And he isn't getting me!'

'Eve——'

'The answer is no, Derek.'

He sighed. 'I don't have the time to argue with you right now, you have to be on stage in a few minutes. And for what it's worth, Eve,' he added almost gently, 'whoever he was, he isn't worth it.'

She froze. 'What do you mean?' she demanded tautly.

'You know what I mean. I've known you almost five

years now, and you've never let a man near you——'

'I've been out on dates!'

'Date, in the singular. You never go out with the same man twice.'

She gave a tight smile. 'Maybe I just like variety.'

Derek shook his head. 'That isn't true and you know it. No man lasts with you because he isn't allowed to get near you, either physically or emotionally.'

Eve flushed. 'You're near me.'

'Only as a friend, and only as near as you'll let me. Eve, you——'

'I have to go, Derek,' she interrupted abruptly. 'But I've never interfered in your private life, and I don't expect you to interfere in mine.'

'Eve——'

'I have to go.' She hurried out of the room as the music began to play.

It was perhaps unfortunate that the first person she saw was Bart Jordan. He was sitting in the front row of the audience, in an end seat, his blond hair very distinctive.

Eve glared at him, her resentment a tangible thing. This man had caused her to argue with Derek, something she never did, and worst of all he had brought back the painful memories of Carl.

If anything her performance was even better than last night, her anticipation of telling Bartholomew Jordan just what she thought of him incentive enough for her to give the performance of a lifetime. She had never been so sensually abandoned during the rock numbers, so heartbreaking during the sad love songs.

By the end of the evening she knew the appreciative clapping and shouting to be wholly deserved, and a lot of the fans were rising to their feet. Only one man didn't applaud; Bartholomew Jordan got up and left by a side door as her last number came to an end.

Eve watched him go with disbelief. She had been conscious of his still figure all through the concert, had tried a little harder with each new song in the hope that he would applaud that one. He never did, just sat watching her steadily with those luminous green eyes.

Eve became more and more frustrated as the evening went on, and those heavy-lidded eyes never left her, a mocking twist to the firm lips that had plundered hers so thoroughly the evening before.

Well, she would show him when he turned up in her dressing-room. If he thought he had had the brush-off last night he would find out what that really meant tonight!

She waited fifteen minutes for him to show up, and when he didn't she knew he must be waiting for her outside. He had probably left early to get his limousine.

But once she got outside there was no limousine, no Bartholomew Jordan. The damned man had genuinely walked out on her concert!

CHAPTER TWO

EVE'S mood was explosive during rehearsals the next day; she was critical of the musicians, until at last one of them shouted back at her. That took her aback, so much so that she was speechless for several minutes.

'Okay, take a break, everyone,' Derek filled in the silence. 'Back on stage in ten minutes. You come with me.' He pulled Eve off the stage and down into her dressing-room. 'Now, what's going on?' he demanded to know.

Her face was flushed. 'You had no need to do that,' she snapped. 'I could handle it.' She pushed her hair back impatiently.

'Maybe you could,' he sighed, 'But I don't think the boys could. You were throwing the proverbial tantrum out there, Eve.'

'I was not——'

'You were, and you still are. What on earth is the matter with you?' he sighed his exasperation. 'You're being hell today!'

She glared at him angrily for several minutes, her expression one of rebellion. Then the fight went out of her. She *was* being hell, she was surprised someone hadn't told her earlier; the boys in the group didn't usually take any nonsense, not from anyone.

'I'll apologise,' she said tautly, her hands thrust into the back pocket of her skin-tight denims, her lemon tee-shirt figure-hugging too.

'That doesn't answer my question,' he said firmly. 'What's upset you?'

'Nothing.'

'Eve!'

She bit her lip, looking down at her hands. She didn't know what was wrong with her, she just felt angry at the whole world. 'Maybe I'm tired,' she shrugged.

'We all are. That's no excuse.' He put his arm about her shoulders. 'You know that, don't you, Eve? Guy was playing that last number perfectly, you were the one off key.'

'I've said I'll apologise!'

He moved back. 'Make sure you do. Having the musicians walk out on us is something I don't need.'

'Derek——'

'Okay, okay,' he held up his hands defensively, shaking his head. 'I don't know you in this mood.'

She didn't know herself. Usually nothing got to her, and yet since her first meeting with Bartholomew Jordan her mood had been very erratic. And no man was allowed to do that to her, *she* wouldn't allow them to.

The rest of the rehearsals went off all right. Guy accepted her apology, but she took all the band out to lunch just to ease things between them. She was behaving very badly, something she had sworn never to do in her career. She was a lone woman working in a male-dominated environment, and the last thing she needed was to earn the reputation of being a temperamental bitch.

Luckily her behaviour didn't seem to have inhibited the men in any way; their jokes were as ribald as usual as they more or less took the local pub over. She felt a little easier when she emerged out into the afternoon sunshine, walking to Derek's flat rather than taking a taxi. She was unrecognisable without her dramatic stage make-up, just another pretty girl enjoying the sunshine.

She was relaxed before the start of that evening's show—always a bad sign. The adrenalin should be pumping, her senses charged and alive. It was almost as if she had burnt herself out in anger that morning, and she had no enthusiasm for the show ahead of her.

'Present for the lovely lady.' Derek appeared in the doorway of her dressing-room, or rather the bottom half of him did; the top half was obscured by a huge bouquet.

She stood up. 'Derek, you shouldn't——'

'I didn't.' He held out the flowers to her.

Eve stiffened. They were roses—red roses. The card clearly said 'Bartholomew'. Her mouth tightened, and she fought down the impulse to throw the flowers away. They were beautiful roses, just in bud, and a deep, deep red. There must be at least three dozen here, she just couldn't destroy them. Maybe one of the stage workers would like them for his wife?

'Is it safe to come in?' Derek raised a hopeful eyebrow.

She laughed at his pretended fear. 'Yes, come in,' she invited, putting the flowers down on the table; the ones from yesterday were still lying there in their cellophane.

Derek strolled over to a chair, leaning his arms on its back. 'Persistent, isn't he?' he said dryly.

Eve gave him an angry glare. 'I suppose you looked at the card,' she accused.

He shrugged. 'I didn't realise it was a secret.'

'It isn't,' she sighed. 'How long have I got?' she changed the subject.

'Five minutes. Are you ready?'

She spun round in the electric blue cat-suit. 'Don't I look ready?' she teased.

'You always look beautiful.'

'Thanks,' she accepted dryly. 'Why the flattery,

Derek?' she asked, eyes narrowed.

'No reason. Surely it can't hurt to make you feel good before you go out on stage? You were looking a bit tired when we arrived,' he added worriedly.

Strange, she didn't feel that way any more; the adrenalin was pumping, the blood heated in her veins. 'I'm fine now, Derek,' she assured him.

'Mood gone?'

'I—Yes, mood gone,' she said reluctantly.

He quirked an eyebrow at the roses. 'He wouldn't have anything to do with that, would he?'

'Certainly not!' Her tone was waspish. 'I wouldn't allow a man like that to affect me in any way.'

'A man like that?'

'Yes, a man like that!' Her eyes flashed deeply blue. 'You know the type as well as I do, Derek. They think their money can buy them anything.'

'He was rich too, was he?'

She gave him a sharp look. 'Who was?'

Derek shook his head and stood up. 'This last few days your guard has really started to slip, Eve. I think maybe Bart Jordan is starting to get to you.'

'No man "gets to me"!' Her expression was fierce.

'Not since the last rich man who let you down, no,' he agreed calmly. 'But everyone has a type they fall for again and again, and I think maybe rich men are your type.'

'I'll show you what I think of rich men!' she told him explosively, picking up the roses and throwing them out into the corridor. 'I'd do the same to Bartholomew Jordan if he was here,' she added childishly, wondering why she was letting a man like Bartholomew Jordan bother her in this way. And he was bothering her.

She meant it when she told Derek that no man got to her—they hadn't, not since Carl. And she wasn't going to let Bartholomew Jordan upset the even tenor of her life. Once she got back to Norfolk she could forget his very existence. In fact she would make sure she did.

She walked out of the dressing-room, her head held high, the crumpled roses completely ignored, forgotten as she stood in the wings waiting to go on stage.

But Carl wasn't forgotten, would never be forgotten. And just making her think of him like this was reason enough to hate Bartholomew Jordan.

She ran out on stage as the music began to play, a bright artificial smile fixed on her lips as she began to sing the first number. Her gaze was drawn reluctantly to the seat Bartholomew Jordan had occupied the night before. It was empty! Not occupied by someone else, but *empty*. What was the man trying to do to her? First of all he sent her roses, then he snubbed her by not turning up to watch her concert. He had to be the holder of that ticket, it was too much of a coincidence for him not to be.

Once again it was her anger towards Bartholomew Jordan that inspired her to give a brilliant performance, and the audience were very appreciative at the interval as she tried to get off the stage.

'Fantastic!' Derek glowed, handing her the glass of fresh orange juice that was all she liked to drink when she was performing.

Eve noticed that the roses were gone from the corridor; they were also noticeably absent from her dressing-room as she slumped down into a chair.

Derek frowned at her paleness. 'Are you feeling all right?' he asked worriedly.

'I—not really,' she admitted dazedly, the charged tension of the last hour and a quarter seeming to have drained her of all her strength. She felt weak, lethargic, and the thought of going back on to that stage stretched like a nightmare in front of her.

'You have to get changed.' Derek stood up to take the red suit out of her wardrobe. 'You only have another ten minutes before you have to go back on stage.'

She fought off feelings of dizziness. 'I—I feel—strange, Derek.'

'Drink some more orange juice,' he encouraged desperately.

She gave a wan smile. 'I don't think that's going to do any good.'

His expression was angrily impatient. 'It has to. You can't let me down now, Eve. I've just about sold my soul for you to do these five concerts.'

'No one asked you to!' Her eyes flashed, deeply blue between thick dark lashes. 'Okay,' she stood up, swaying slightly, pushing back the feelings of faintness, 'you go out, I'll get changed.'

'I'll help you——'

'You damn well won't!' she snapped. 'I've been dressing myself since I was three years old, I don't need any help.'

'Maybe that's your trouble, Eve,' he stormed over to the door. 'You won't accept help from anyone. No one can go through life independent of other human warmth.'

'I can,' she glared at him. 'Now get out of here.'

'Don't worry, I'm going!' He slammed the door so hard behind him the whole room seemed to shake.

Oh dear, what had she done! Derek was the one true friend she had, and she had just thrown him out of her dressing-room.

She ran to the door, wrenching it open. 'Derek!' she cried after him as he walked away from her. 'Derek, please,' she begged.

He turned slowly, his face stony. 'Yes?' he asked curtly.

'Oh, Derek, I'm sorry!' She held out her hand pleadingly.

For a moment it seemed he was going to ignore that plea, then he relented and gave a rueful smile. 'Our first argument.' He shrugged. 'Not bad after five years.'

'I really am sorry,' she bit her lip. 'I don't know what's wrong with me.'

'Nerves,' he dismissed. 'Hurry and change, Eve. Only another hour to go and then you can sleep for twelve hours if you want to.'

'Tomorrow's rehearsal . . .?'

'Forget it. You couldn't be any better than you are right now. And I happen to think you need the rest more. Just get through this hour, Eve, and you can take tomorrow off.'

'All right,' she nodded, her smile bright, but that smile faded as she went back into her room.

She was trembling all over, her skin cold and clammy. Something was wrong, seriously wrong, and yet she knew she couldn't let Derek down. Derek? Shouldn't she be going through this gruelling torture for herself, and not because of loyalty to Derek?

She knew he wasn't lying when he said he had just about sold his soul to get the money together for this weekly booking. She had had one hit record, her second was slowly starting to creep up the charts, but that didn't make her a star. Backers for a relative new-comer weren't easy to come by, and it had taken Derek months of hard work to get the cash together.

And now she wished it were all over, wished she never had to perform in front of an audience again. She loved to sing, had always enjoyed it, but maybe the reviewers were right when they said she didn't have the stamina to compete in the big time.

It took all her will-power to change into the red suit, but her entrance back on stage was greeted with ecstatic applause. She was halfway through the first number when the spotlights playing across the stage picked up the fair head set at an arrogant angle on the first row of seats, the bright light emphasising the many shades of blond.

Bartholomew Jordan was now sitting in the seat he had reserved! He must have come in during the interval. She hadn't spotted him at first because it just hadn't occurred to her that he would arrive this late in the show.

But there he was, just as self-assured as ever, looking totally out of place amongst the teenage audience she had attracted, the deep green velvet jacket, snowy white shirt, and black trousers equally out of place. He looked as if he were either on his way to, or had just come from, a dinner engagement.

Once again he didn't applaud her performance, but his green-eyed gaze didn't deviate from her once as she sang song after song. This time he stayed until the end of the concert, but he made no effort to come backstage to see her.

Eve had to admit to being puzzled by his behaviour. He obviously hadn't lost interest in her, and yet he wasn't pursuing her as doggedly as she would have expected him to. Not like Carl; he had been very persistent. But she hadn't been so unwilling then, hadn't got her fingers burnt.

Carl. She would never forget him, or the lesson he had taught her. Her mind was plagued with thoughts of him as she tried in vain to fall asleep that night. She was exhausted, she should have fallen asleep instantly, but memories of Carl wouldn't be denied. She could see him now, tall, dark, incredibly handsome, with a lethal charm that no woman, least of all the naïve fool she had been then, could resist.

She had been singing in a club out of town the first time she saw him, singing the meaningless songs that didn't intrude on the enjoyment of the patrons as they ate their meal before going in to gamble on the gaming tables in the other room.

Carl had been with a tall blonde woman, classically beautiful, her clothes obviously having an exclusive label. And yet for all her apparent wealth and beauty the other woman hadn't been able to hold Carl's attention; Eve had done that.

The intensity of his gaze made her blush, and she even stumbled a couple of times over the songs she had been singing night after night for the past two weeks, ever since the club had opened. She had been lucky to get the job in the first place, although she was far from being the top entertainment the club had to offer, the top stars appearing in the gaming-room.

Carl had come back the next night, alone this time. He had invited her over to have a drink with him during her break. She had refused, as the club rules said that she wasn't to mix socially with the customers. She had been grateful enough for this stipulation when she first went to work at the club; a lot of the places she had worked in in the past had treated her as little more than a call-girl. And yet she had been attracted to Carl, had wanted to be with him, had been regretful at having to turn him down.

He had finally realised what the problem was and had arranged to meet her away from the club, although he usually managed to get into the club to see her for a few minutes each evening when she was working. That first evening they had gone out for a late supper. Carl had got her to talk about her family, about her dead parents, the godparents who had brought her up since their death. He had seemed genuinely interested in her life, although he revealed little about himself, except that his name was Carl Prentiss, and that he had a business in the City.

Eve had been naïve, naïve and totally stupid, infatuated with a surface charm and the way he received only the best service wherever they went together. His affluence was something he took for granted, but something that in her naïveté she had been impressed with.

When he kissed her goodnight he never took advantage of her eagerness, another clever move on his part, she now realised. She would have run a mile if she had known of his true interest regarding her.

She could still remember that last painful scene between them, when she had learnt exactly what Carl wanted from her.

They had been seeing each other for about two months by this time, meeting one or two evenings a week. Carl often took her to dinner after she had finished work. By this time she was so much in love with him, with his confidence, his maturity, that when he had told her he had a present for her, a surprise present, she had instantly thought of an engagement ring, of marriage.

'I've found you an apartment,' he told her once they were out in his car, a Porsche, its sleek lines telling of its price. Carl told her he had had it custom-built, and she could believe that; the car was the last thing in luxury.

She had blinked up at him dazedly. 'An apartment?'

'Mm,' he nodded, his smile at its most persuasive, his handsome face flushed with pleasure. 'Somewhere we can go to be alone.'

'But——' she frowned, her disappointment about the engagement ring very acute, 'I already have an apartment.'

'With four other girls!' he scoffed. 'I said somewhere we can be alone, Eve. And I do want to be alone with you, darling,' his hand came out to grasp her thigh, his fingers lightly caressing through the thin material of her skirt. 'Completely alone,' he added throatily.

'But I can't afford an apartment of my own.' Surely he wasn't suggesting they moved in together! It might be prudish, and totally out of fashion, but she believed a wedding should come before she lived with any man.

Carl turned to smile at her. 'The rent's very cheap, darling,' he assured her. 'And it means I'll be able to visit you there whenever I can get away from the office.'

'And when I'm not at work myself,' she put in worriedly, a little overwhelmed with the speed with which things were moving. So far she had only received goodnight kisses, and now it seemed Carl intended spending a lot of time with her in the privacy of an apartment he had found for her.

Nevertheless, she had been delighted with the apartment, with its location overlooking the river, with the furniture Carl assured her came in with the modest rent. The rent had finally been the deciding point, that and the way Carl had made love to her more intimately than any other man. She had made an embarrassed comment about the size of the bed that occupied the only bedroom, and Carl had wanted to demonstrate that it was only just big enough—for the two of them.

She had only panicked when it seemed he wasn't going to bring an end to their caresses until they had made love fully, and she pulled out of his arms to get up from the bed. Carl had laughed throatily, lying back on the bed to watch her with taunting eyes.

She should have realised then, should have known his intention was to share the apartment with her when he could get away from his *wife*.

She had had no knowledge of Carl's being married, had been shocked to the core when he had arrived at the apartment a couple of days later informing her that he could spend the evening with her as his wife had gone to her parents' and taken the children with her.

Eve had been aghast, horror-stricken with the easy way he told her of his wife and children.

'But I thought you loved me,' she choked. 'I thought you wanted to marry *me*.'

His mouth turned back in a sneer. '*Marry you?*' he scorned. 'Men like me don't marry girls like you.'

'Girls like me . . .?' she echoed faintly.

'Oh, come on, darling,' he smiled mockingly. 'You knew what I was after from the first, you just held back because you wanted more for what you're about to give me.'

'Get out of here!' she screamed at him. 'Get out and don't come back.' She turned away, deep sobs racking her body. Married! Carl was *married*!

He swung her round, his handsome face now an ugly mask, his blue eyes scornful. 'If anyone goes, Eve,' he snarled, 'it will be you. This happens to be my apartment.'

All colour left her face. 'Y-Yours? But I—I pay the rent. I——'

His mocking laughter cut her off mid-sentence. 'Rent! You call that pittance you pay *rent*?'

'Well, yes. I——'

'Grow up, Eve,' he scorned. 'An apartment in this area, *this* apartment, would cost ten times what you're paying.' He pulled her into his arms. 'Don't be difficult, darling,' his lips were at her throat. 'Let's not waste any more of the evening arguing——'

Eve struggled to escape from the arms that were suddenly repugnant to her. 'That woman——' she breathed. 'The one you were with that first evening——'

'My wife,' he said impatiently, his hands pulling at the blouse she wore with a black flower-print skirt, ripping the silky material in his haste.

Eve felt sick, swallowing down the nausea. 'Let me go!' she pushed at his arms ineffectually, feeling her blouse rip even further as Carl became increasingly angry with her. 'Let me go, Carl!' she choked, deathly white.

'What the hell is the matter with you?' He suddenly thrust her away from him. 'You knew the score the day you decided to move in here. Oh, I know you like to keep up an act——'

'Act?' she repeated faintly, slumping down on to the sofa, pulling her torn blouse over her lace-covered breasts, colour flooding her cheeks as Carl clearly mocked the action.

'The act of the sweet little virgin,' his mouth twisted. 'The Miss Butter-wouldn't-melt-in-your-mouth act,' he scoffed.

Eve looked up at him with pained eyes, wondering how she had ever thought herself in love with this monster of a man, a man devoid of all sensitivity, a man who cared nothing for her as a person but only wanted her body, inexperienced as it was.

'How can you say that?' she gasped. 'I am a virgin.'

'I know that, Eve,' he taunted. 'But you weren't exactly backward in coming forward the last time we were here together.' He sat down on the sofa beside her, pulling her determinedly towards him. 'You're a passionate little thing,' he mocked, 'and after a few more lessons from me you might be able to please me as much as I please you.' He laughed softly, standing up to lift her effortlessly into his arms and walk purposefully into the bedroom. 'I think it's time you had another lesson. You might be less prudish afterwards.'

'No!' She pushed at him, his arms tightening like steel bands about her. Carl was surprisingly strong, well muscled, and kept that way by a work-out in a gymnasium three times a week. Now he exerted that strength, throwing her down on the bed and swiftly following her, holding her down with his leg over hers, his arm across her breasts as his mouth plundered hers.

Eve felt nauseous, fighting him for all she was worth. But he wouldn't stop, and his hands quickly dispensed with her clothes, much to her shame and embarrassment. When his mouth moved to her breasts she knew she couldn't stand it any more, and her nails dug into his back. Carl stiffened, groaning in his throat, finding pleasure in the pain she was inflicting.

'You're learning,' he chuckled throatily. 'I like that,' he moaned. 'Do it again, little wildcat.'

She felt like screaming, almost hysterical by this time, and her hand went up to scrape her nails down his tanned cheek.

He sprang back in pain, his hand going up to his face. 'You little bitch!' His face contorted viciously, his hand coming away from his cheek covered in blood, four livid scratches marring his skin, blood still slowly seeping down his bronzed cheek. 'You little bitch,' he repeated, and his hand came out to land painfully against the side of her face.

'Carl . . .!' She cringed back against the pillows, terrified of the burning anger that tautened every muscle of his body.

'Yes—Carl,' he snarled. 'How the hell do you suppose I'm going to explain these scratches to my wife?' He took her by the shoulders. 'You stupid damned bitch! Stupid, stupid, stupid!' He flung her back against the pillows. 'Well, you'll pay for it now!'

What had followed had been the most humiliating

experience of her life. Her body had been subjected to Carl's lovemaking in the most brutal way possible, her brain numbed, the bruises on her body and mind not felt until much later.

When he had finished with her he stood up to dress, not even looking at her as she huddled beneath the sheet, her body bruised all over from his rough treatment of her.

He knotted his tie with meticulous care, once again the debonair man he had been when he arrived an hour ago. God, she thought, had it only been an hour! It had seemed like an endless nightmare, leaving her with her body violated. But the scratches she had given him made him a marked man.

He seemed to think so too, as he studied them in the mirror, a dark scowl to his face. 'Helen will give me hell about this,' he muttered furiously, turning to glare at Eve. 'What the hell am I supposed to tell her?'

She was sobbing quietly, feeling as if her body were unclean. 'Why don't you tell her the truth?' she said dully.

He gave a tight smile. 'That a little wildcat scratched me? I think she'll guess that. It wasn't a very wise thing to do, Eve, Helen's family have some important connections. I'll have to do penance for weeks to make up for this.' He sat down on the bed, lightly touching her cheek before she flinched away. 'It probably means I won't be able to see you for a few weeks, just until the hue and cry dies down.'

Eve recoiled from his touch, her disgust for him evident in her eyes. 'You mean you—you intend coming back here?'

'Of course,' he laughed throatily. 'You were a bit rough tonight, Eve, but I liked it.'

'*I* was rough?' she gasped.

'Okay, I was too,' he shrugged. 'But you started it.'

He kissed her hard on the mouth before standing up. 'I'll call you when I can manage to get away. Take care, hmm?' He walked confidently out of the room.

'Carl . . .?' she called after him, but he seemed not to hear her, and the door closed quietly as he left.

How long she lay there in frozen silence she never afterwards knew, and then suddenly she began to cry, deep pain-racked sobs that shook her whole body.

And her humiliation hadn't been over either; there had been much more to come, humiliation of another kind this time.

She had finally fallen asleep in the early hours of the morning, just too weary to leave at that time, confident in the knowledge that Carl wouldn't be back tonight. She had been woken by the insistent ringing of the doorbell, and pulled on her robe and went to answer the door. It couldn't be Carl; he would never ring, she had discovered yesterday that he had his own key.

A delivery boy stood outside, a huge bouquet of red roses in his hand. 'Miss Meredith?' he asked brightly.

She clutched her robe to her, aware of how bedraggled she must look, the cut and swelling on the side of her mouth making it look as if someone had punched her, bruises on her arms and throat.

'Yes?' Her voice came out husky, her throat sore from all the crying she had done during the night; she seemed to have cried even in her sleep.

'These are for you.' The boy held out the roses, waiting expectantly.

Eve took them dazedly, turning back into the room to find her purse, handing the boy a tip before slowly closing the door.

The roses were from Carl, of course, an apology for his behaviour the night before. 'Sorry, darling,' the card read. 'I love you. Call you soon.'

He *loved* her, after the way he had treated her? His

idea of love and hers differed greatly, and the sooner she got away from him and out of this apartment the better she would feel. She left the roses on the table untouched, then called Rosemary, one of her old roommates.

Of course she could sleep over with them, Rosemary had assured her, although she would have to sleep on the sofa, as they had already let her old room. Eve hadn't cared where she slept, it could have been on the floor for all she cared, as long as it wasn't in this apartment, like the kept woman she undoubtedly was.

She was halfway through packing when she heard the key in the lock. Carl! Heavens, he was back already! What was she going to say to him? What could she do?

She wiped her hands nervously down her denims, looking very young and vulnerable as she walked out into the lounge. She gasped as she saw the woman who stood there. Helen Prentiss, Carl's wife!

The woman turned, cool blue eyes raking over Eve's casual appearance with obvious disdain. Her own appearance was impeccable, from her sleek shoulder-length hair to the pale blue leather shoes that exactly matched the colour of the fitted blue dress she wore.

She arched an eyebrow at Eve, glancing fleetingly at the roses, her mouth twisting derisively. 'Miss Meredith?' she drawled, her voice huskily attractive, her precise English accent obviously acquired at a private school.

Eve licked her lips, wondering when this nightmare was going to end, or if indeed it ever would. 'Yes,' she confirmed shakily.

Helen Prentiss picked up the card that lay beside the roses. 'So I see,' she scorned. '*He's* sorry?' she said with amusement. 'After the mess you made of his face I would have thought you would be the contrite one.' Hard blue eyes suddenly probed Eve's pale face.

'You're the one who did that to Carl, aren't you? My God,' she gave an abrupt laugh, 'don't tell me he's cheated on both of us!'

'No,' Eve bit her bottom lip, 'I—I did it.'

'Really?' Those hard blue eyes narrowed, a frown marring the beautiful face. 'Strange, you don't look the violent type. Oh well,' she shrugged in a bored voice, 'you never can tell. Would you mind if I sat down?' she asked calmly.

'I—No. Go ahead,' Eve invited awkwardly.

The other woman did so, crossing one shapely leg over the other. She was a really beautiful woman, aged about thirty, and Eve couldn't understand why Carl felt the need to be unfaithful to her.

Helen Prentiss looked up at her. 'Now what do you intend to do about my husband?'

Again Eve licked her dry lips. 'D-Do?' she repeated, shaking her head. 'I don't know what you mean.'

The other woman sighed. 'How old are you, my dear?'

'Almost twenty,' she answered awkwardly.

'You're the youngest to date,' Helen Prentiss drawled in that bored voice.

'Youngest . . .?' Eve repeated dazedly.

'Yes.' The other woman gave an amused laugh. 'You don't think you're the first, do you?'

'I—Well, I—I hadn't——'

'Hadn't thought about it,' the other woman finished dryly. 'Well, to my knowledge you're the sixth one in this apartment.'

Oh God! Eve dropped into a chair, feeling suddenly faint. She wasn't even the first woman Carl had kept in this way, she was just one in a long line, although by the determined tilt of Helen Prentiss's chin she could be the last.

She frowned. 'Don't you mind?'

Helen Prentiss shrugged. 'The first dozen or so times I did, now I'm past caring. But I have the children to think of. I wouldn't want them to know what a bastard their father is.'

'I—How old are they, your children?'

'Nine, six, and four. The last two were attempts at reconciliations,' Helen explained bitterly. 'Not very successful ones.' She snapped open her handbag, and took out her cheque-book. 'Now, how much do you want to disappear from my husband's life?' She held a gold pen poised ready to write.

Eve went even paler, standing agitatedly to her feet. 'I don't want any money,' she choked. 'I'm leaving anyway. I was just packing when you arrived.'

'Very well.' Helen Prentiss put the cheque-book away, standing gracefully to her feet. She stopped at the door, her expression softening somewhat. 'I'm sorry I had to do this, Miss Meredith.'

She shook her head. 'You didn't do anything—I told you, I was leaving anyway.'

Helen Prentiss nodded, her blue eyes shadowed. 'He's a brute, isn't he?' she said resignedly, and left as silently as she had arrived.

Eve must have broken all records packing her suitcase and leaving that hateful apartment. Carl had telephoned her several times at the flat, had even come round himself once, only to be turned away by an angry Rosemary.

Yes, she had learnt her lesson about men the hard way, but she *had* learnt it.

And now she had another spoilt rich man pursuing her, a man who also sent red roses. But Bartholomew Jordan wasn't going to get anywhere with her, she would make very sure of that.

CHAPTER THREE

Eve slept in late the next morning as Derek had said she could, spending a leisurely hour in the bath once she got up. Would Bartholomew Jordan be there again tonight? She had a feeling he would be.

The roses arrived as usual, signed 'Bart?' this time. She had to admire his nerve!

Yes, he was there as she began the concert, his behaviour exactly the same as before, those steady green eyes enigmatic as he watched her. This time he stayed for the full concert, getting up and leaving only as the rest of the audience applauded.

Eve had felt better tonight, although the feeling of weakness once again washed over her as she left the stage, and that cold clammy feeling was back. Derek caught her as she swayed.

'What is it?' he asked worriedly, looking down at her pale face.

'I—I don't know,' she managed to murmur through suddenly stiff lips, the world suddenly seeming very far away, everything looking as if it was at the far end of a telescope. 'I feel—weird.'

'I would say Miss Meredith is suffering from strain.' Bartholomew Jordan spoke authoritatively from behind them, instantly taking charge of the situation. 'Have my car brought round to the back entrance,' he ordered Derek. 'I'm taking Eve home.'

'No!' She struggled to free herself as Bartholomew Jordan took over her support, his arm about her waist as he led her effortlessly down to her dressing-room. 'My car should be here in a moment,' he told her as he lowered her into a chair, his quick gaze taking in everything about the room at a glance, the roses he had sent still in their Cellophane wrapping.

Her legs and arms felt so heavy, her whole body lethargic, the world fading and returning in waves. She was even too weary to fight this man as he seemed to take control, of her and the situation.

He came down on his haunches in front of her, rubbing her chilled hands, very attractive in a dark evening suit that made his hair appear even more golden, his tan even deeper. 'How long have you been like this?' he demanded in that husky voice that spoke of authority.

She shook her head, trying to clear the fog that seemed to be taking over her brain. 'I—Only just now,' she licked her lips, their dryness making it difficult for her to speak. 'I—I was fine—out there,' she waved her hand in the general direction of the stage.

His eyes were narrowed to green slits. 'You looked far from fine to me. You've been bordering on this collapse for days,' he added grimly.

'I didn't collapse!' she roused herself enough to protest. 'I'm just tired, that's all.'

'Like hell you are!' he exploded, standing up forcefully. 'Derek had no business letting you continue in this state.'

Her eyes sparkled deeply blue as she fought back the fog that threatened to overtake her. 'It wasn't a case of "letting" me do anything, Mr Jordan. I'm twenty-five years of age, I control my own life, my own actions. And I can find my own way home!'

'You can take your choice, Eve,' he said hardly. 'You either go by ambulance or in my car.'

'I'm going by car——'

'Then I'm taking you,' he told her firmly, his tone brooking no argument.

'I don't want you to. I——' Suddenly she started to cry, frowning surprise at her own weakness. What on earth was the matter with her? She never cried, never!

But she was crying now, the mascara that was supposed to be waterproof running in black streaks down her white cheeks. And she couldn't stop herself, crying and crying, until her body shuddered with exhaustion.

Bartholomew Jordan grasped the tops of her arms and shook her gently. 'Stop it, Eve,' he ordered in a commanding voice. 'Come on, pull yourself together.'

'Pull myself together?' She began to pummel his chest with her fists. 'It's all your fault, all your fault!' she accused brokenly, collapsing against his chest.

Derek appeared in the open doorway, frowning his concern. 'The car is here,' he told Bartholomew Jordan vaguely, his attention on Eve as she huddled against the other man. 'Eve . . .?'

'Leave her,' Bart ordered, swinging her up into his arms and striding over to the door. 'I'll want to talk to you later,' he muttered to Derek, his expression grim.

He was infinitely gentle as he made her comfortable in the back of the car, tucking a blanket about her suddenly cold body.

'Here, you'll need this.' Derek handed him the key to his flat. 'I can use Judy's,' he added, his worried gaze fixed on Eve's still form.

'Judy?' the other man rasped.

'My wife. We'll be along later. I just have to settle things here first.'

Bartholomew Jordan nodded tersely. 'Very well. I'll stay with Eve until you arrive home.' He climbed into the car next to Eve, at once pulling her into the protective curve of his arm.

She didn't have any fight left in her, finding comfort in the even rise and fall of his chest, his aftershave sharp and tangy, a nice smell, as was the aroma of the cheroots he smoked.

She snuggled against his firm warmth, just wanting to rest for a while. He was warm, warm and comfortable, and . . . When she woke up the limousine had come to a halt outside Derek's apartment building and Bartholomew Jordan was lifting her out of the car.

'I can walk,' she told him weakly.

'I'm sure you can.' His face was only inches away from her own as he carried her inside, the cleft in his strong chin on a level with her ruffled dark hair.

Adam accompanied them, dismissed back to the car once he had unlocked the flat door and switched on the lights.

'Which room?' Bart asked her abruptly.

'That one.' She lifted her head long enough to point him in the right direction, dropping back weakly into his arms once the deed had been done.

He marched into the bedroom, not seeming to be bothered by having already carried her up three flights of stairs, the muscles in his arms and chest flexed tautly against her. He lowered her down on to the bed. 'I presume Derek and his wife have the other bedroom,' he said dryly.

'Yes,' she admitted huskily.

His mouth twisted derisively. 'So he isn't your lover?' he taunted.

'Certainly not!' she replied indignantly.

His mouth quirked into a smile now, the harshness that surrounded him like a cloak instantly dispersing. 'But you enjoyed letting me think he was,' he drawled.

'Why not?' she snapped irritably. 'It was what you wanted to believe.'

He gave a husky laugh. 'You know damn well it wasn't,' he chided softly. 'Which room is the bathroom?' he asked briskly.

Eve frowned. 'Next door,' she told him in a puzzled voice.

He nodded. 'I'll be back in a moment.'

He was gone more than a moment, finally coming back with a flannel and towel, sitting down on the side of the bed to slowly wash her face with meticulous care. Eve struggled against this added humiliation, but Bart just gave a soft triumphant laugh.

When he had finished he sat back with a satisfied smile on his face. 'You look wonderfully sexy with all that make-up on,' he told her huskily. 'But without it you look—beautiful.'

She turned her face into the pillow, feeling suddenly stripped naked. 'I look sixteen,' she mumbled, wishing she had the strength to get away from this man, or at least the words to make him leave.

'Exactly,' he nodded. 'This is the real you.'

'I'm *all* the real me!' She looked up at him defiantly. 'And as you've started you may as well finish,' she snapped. 'You'll find some cream and cotton-wool in the bathroom cabinet—I need them to stop my skin drying out,' she explained. 'No matter how men like to believe women have naturally soft skin we usually need a helping hand,' she added derisively.

Long tapered fingers came out to smooth her peachy-cream cheeks. 'You have wonderful skin, Eve,' he murmured, his head bending slightly as he kissed her slowly on the cheek. He sat back, grinning widely. 'Before you put all that gunk on it,' he teased before disappearing into the bathroom again, coming back with the requested cream and cotton-wool.

Eve was aware of him watching her as she deftly cleansed and creamed her skin, her cheeks bright red from the kiss he had just given her. No man had ever kissed her like that before, an undemanding brotherly kiss.

'Thank you,' she said huskily as he disposed of the cream and cotton-wool.

'Now for the clothes.' He returned determinedly to the bed.

'No!' She cringed back against the pillows, her arms folded defensively across her body. 'I can do that myself. I'm grateful for your help, but——'

'We can talk about gratitude some other time,' he dismissed. 'Right now you're going to get undressed and then you're going to sleep.' He helped her to sit up, unzipping the front of the blue cat-suit.

'Stop it!' Her hands covered the nakedness of her breasts, the snug fit of the cat-suit not allowing for underwear. 'I can do this myself,' she protested at his insistence.

He pulled the suit down to her waist with cool detachment. 'I've seen a woman's body before,' he taunted. 'And not all of them as skinny as you,' he told her as he pulled the suit off completely.

She glared up at him. 'I am not skinny!'

'You are, you know,' he frowned as he looked down at her naked body. 'Much too thin,' he added almost to himself. 'Where's your nightgown?'

Eve hastily covered herself with the quilt. 'Under the pillow,' she muttered.

'Lift up, then,' he ordered. 'And for goodness' sake stop acting like an outraged virgin. I doubt I'm the first man to see you without your clothes.'

Colour flooded her cheeks. Only Carl had ever seen her naked, and he hadn't been interested in admiring her body but in possessing it. He had only wanted to hurt her, and he had done that, so much so that she had never wanted another man to see her naked again. And now Bartholomew Jordan was looking down at her with calm green eyes, her lack of clothing meaning nothing to him. Except to tell her she was too skinny!

She sat up, her mouth set stubbornly. 'I can put my own nightgown on, thank you.'

'Yes.' But he still put the cotton nightgown over her head, pulling it down to cover her body.

'Shouldn't you be getting home to your wife, Mr Jordan?' she snapped as he looked mockingly at the sack-like nightgown. 'I'm sure her night attire is infinitely more attractive than mine,' she added waspishly.

One eyebrow quirked with amusement. 'I don't have a wife, Eve,' he drawled. 'But if I did her night attire would consist of—me,' he finished softly.

'Oh!' She blushed fiery red; his meaning was blatantly clear. 'I—I thought you would be married,' she said to cover her embarrassment.

His mouth twisted. 'I haven't fallen into that trap yet, no.' His eyes narrowed. 'Is that why you've been rejecting my flowers?'

Her expression was fierce. 'I happen to hate red roses!' she told him vehemently.

Bartholomew Jordan gave a short amused laugh. 'That never occurred to me. I thought all women liked red roses.'

'I don't!'

'So it was the flowers you disliked, and not me?'

'I wouldn't say that,' she said dryly, eyeing him mockingly.

'Would you like an apology for the other night?' he queried softly, moving to sit on the side of the bed again.

'An apology?' She blinked her bewilderment, wishing he would move away from her. He was an overwhelming individual, sensually so, and she didn't like him this close to her.

Bart nodded. 'I was rude to you, crudely rude. Not that it isn't true about my wanting you,' he told her seriously. 'But I had no reason to suppose you even liked me, let alone that you would go to bed with me.'

Eve frowned, not trusting his sudden change of attitude at all. This man was determined, ruthlessly so, and this could just be another way of getting his own way. 'I'm tired,' she told him distantly. 'I'd like to go to sleep now.'

'Of course.' He bent and kissed her lightly on the brow. 'You aren't strong enough for this sort of life,' he said softly.

She shrugged. 'I only have one more night to go.'

Bart frowned. 'I don't think you'll make it.'

'I have to,' she said simply.

He tucked the blankets more firmly about her. 'I think I hear Derek.' He stopped at the door. 'Will you let me come and see you tomorrow?'

She looked at his hard face, the determined chin, the firm mouth, the unflinching eyes, and knew he rarely asked in this way. He was a man who took, who acted without questioning, used to a wealth of authority, his orders carried out at a glance. And yet with her he had asked, possibly because he realised his autocratic behaviour wouldn't get him anywhere with her.

'If you want to,' she shrugged dismissively. 'But I'll be better by then.'

'I doubt it.' His eyes narrowed grimly. 'I'll be here about eleven o'clock.' He opened the door.

'But no roses?' she reminded him hastily.

He turned back to smile at her. 'No roses,' he promised, softly closing the door behind him.

Judy came in a few minutes later, very concerned as she looked down at Eve's face, almost as white as the sheet, her dark hair splayed out across the pillow.

'How are you, love?' she asked worriedly.

'Better.' Eve gave a wan smile. 'Ba—er—Mr Jordan has been very helpful,' she admitted grudgingly.

Judy's eyebrows rose as she took in Eve's appearance. 'He did this?'

Colour flooded her cheeks. Judy was as much aware as Derek how Eve kept men out of her life, and yet now it looked to all intents and purposes as if she had calmly allowed Bartholomew Jordan to undress her. She had been too weak to stop him, but even if she hadn't been she doubted much would stop that man. He oozed power, over his own life and others.

She grimaced up at Judy. 'I didn't have much choice in the matter.'

'A bit forceful, isn't he?'

'A bit!' Eve derided.

'I'll leave you to rest now,' Judy smiled. 'Derek will probably be in in a moment.'

Eve nodded, glad of the intervening time to think over exactly what had happened to her tonight. That the hard work of the last few months was finally taking its toll was obvious, but what she was going to do about it she just didn't know. Derek had gone to such a lot of work himself to get her this far, if she let him down now he might just decide she wasn't worth the trouble.

She didn't even know if that would be a bad thing. The idea of going back to her home in Norfolk, writing a few songs to get her by money-wise, and singing for her own pleasure as she had used to, suddenly seemed very inviting. It was ungrateful of her, but maybe she wasn't cut out for this life, the sheer hard work, the grabbing meals when you had the time, or when you thought about it.

And then there had been Bartholomew Jordan. His sudden appearance backstage tonight, the way he had taken control, hadn't exactly been a surprise. But his gentleness just now had been, as had his apology. But she had learnt well not to trust men like him, knew from experience that the gentleness just hid his desire, that he hoped to get her defences down enough to make another move in that direction.

Why did he have to be interested in her, why couldn't he choose another woman for his attentions, a woman who was equally interested in him? No doubt he had thought she would be in the beginning, and when she had shown she wasn't she had only made him all the more determined. The same thing had happened so many times in the past that she should have known what to expect. Admittedly most of the other men hadn't been rich enough to shower her with flowers every minute of the day, but Bartholomew Jordan's wealth just made him all the more sure he would win in the end.

She was glad of Derek's entrance to stop her thinking of Bartholomew Jordan, finding herself alternately angry and mystified about him. And she didn't see why she should even be wasting her time thinking about him. After tomorrow night she would be leaving London, and would, she hoped, never see Bartholomew Jordan again.

'He's gone.' Derek saw her frowning glance towards the door. He grimaced. 'He was furious with me.'

Eve's eyes widened. 'But why?' she gasped.

Derek shrugged. 'For letting you go on tonight. I had to tell him about your feeling dizzy last night,' he explained ruefully. 'He said I was damned stupid letting you go on again after that.'

Angry colour darkened her cheeks, her eyes sparkling rebelliously. 'What the hell business is it of his?' she exploded.

'Naturally he's interested——'

'Why naturally?' she glared. 'Just because the man wants to go to bed with me it doesn't mean he can suddenly start to take over my life. God, I'll be glad when tomorrow's show is over and I can get back to normality. It will be nice to get back to nice honest people—you and Judy excepted, of course.'

'Wasn't Jordan honest enough for you?' he teased.

'Too honest. And I didn't mean that sort of honesty. I meant down-to-earth day-to-day living. I can't stand the falseness here, Derek, the stabbing in the back.' She sighed. 'The wisest thing I ever did was move back to Norfolk.'

'Jordan said I was to let you rest, so I'd better go——'

'What's the matter with you, Derek?' she demanded impatiently. 'Since when did you start taking orders from Bartholomew Jordan?'

He flushed uncomfortably. 'It isn't a question of taking orders—looking at you I can see the man's right. And no more arguments,' he added firmly as she went to speak again. 'After a run-in with Jordan I'm in the mood to argue with anyone—and enjoy winning.'

'Who says you would win?' she asked with a return of her old spirit. 'I just had a run-in with him too, remember?'

Derek grinned. 'Nevertheless, you're going to sleep now. Tomorrow we'll get a doctor out to you.'

'I don't need—Don't tell me,' she sighed angrily. 'Bartholomew Jordan's orders?'

'You guessed it,' he smiled ruefully. 'And no one wins an argument with him.'

'I did.' But had she? She thought she had at the time, but now she wasn't so sure. He was still in her life, very much so, still telling everyone what to do and when to do it.

'Sleep tight,' Derek said softly as he closed the door.

That wasn't so easy once she actually tried to do it. Carl had been too much on her mind today, disturbing and upsetting her. She had seen him once more after the night he had taken her so forcibly. She had been out with Derek celebrating some minor booking triumph or other, she couldn't even remember now, and Carl had walked into the club she and Derek were at.

It had been two years since their last meeting, and she had grown up a lot during that time, her naïveté replaced by a wall of hardness that no man could penetrate—and still no man had. Then why did the thought of Bart Jordan keep coming into her mind? He was like a bulldozer—and didn't bulldozers knock down walls?

Carl had looked just the same, the charm still there as he chatted to his own dining companion. But he had seemed bored, restless, his gaze passing over the other people dining, his eyes widening as he saw and recognised Eve.

She had felt as if he were slowly undressing her, aware that her new slenderness emphasised the fullness of her breasts, that the way she now wore her long hair loose instead of secured at her nape gave her a wild gypsyish look. But she no longer looked or dressed to please herself when she was out, she had an image to create. And that Carl had liked that image had been obvious.

Derek had left her briefly a few minutes later to use the telephone, and Carl had taken this opportunity to come over and speak to her.

'Well, well, well,' he drawled appreciatively as he sat down.

'Yes, I am, thank you,' she deliberately misunderstood him, her gaze steady.

Carl grinned. 'You look fantastic!'

'Yes,' she accepted calmly.

His amusement deepened. 'You've grown up, Eve.'

She nodded. 'A little late, but yes. Now would you

mind, I'm here with someone...' she told him pointedly. 'And so are you.'

He didn't move, his gaze warm as he looked at the low cleavage on the skinny-rib top she wore. 'I can put Barbara in a taxi,' he said softly, moving closer, his arm across the back of her chair. 'Can you get rid of the man you're with?' His fingers trailed lightly down her bare arm.

She moved away from him. 'I have no wish to "get rid" of Derek,' she said stiffly. 'But I wish *you* would go away.'

Her reluctance had only seemed to make him more interested. 'I'm not married now, Eve,' he breathed huskily against her earlobe. 'So you don't need to worry about that any more.'

'I'm not worried, Carl,' she told him coldly, wondering what on earth had happened to Derek; he seemed to have been gone for hours, although she felt sure it was only minutes. 'Although I'm glad your wife finally had the sense to divorce you.'

His face darkened angrily. 'Still a bitch, aren't you, Eve?' He sat away from her. 'I couldn't give a damn about losing Helen and that interfering family of hers— but I miss my children,' he added fiercely.

Eve looked at him calmly, seeing the pain etched beside his nose and mouth. It was reassuring to know that he cared for something else beside himself. 'Maybe you should have thought of that earlier,' she said callously, her hatred towards this man as strong as ever.

His fingers dug into her arms as he pulled her savagely towards him, his face only inches away from her own. 'You cold little bitch!' he snarled.

She looked at him steadily. 'It's better than being the bastard you are.'

'You——'

'Everything okay?' Derek miraculously appeared at the table.

Carl had stood up and walked away without another word, pulling the protesting Barbara to her feet and leaving.

'He looked as if he was being nasty.' Derek frowned at her pale face.

Eve shrugged. 'Nothing I couldn't handle.'

Derek nodded. 'Carl Prentiss is one of the men to avoid in this world.'

Her eyes widened. 'You know him?'

'Who doesn't?' he dismissed. 'But I'm glad you didn't like him, he means trouble.'

Derek had dismissed the whole incident as just another pick-up. He had no idea of the part Carl had played in her past, and she hadn't enlightened him, the painful episode with Carl was buried deep in her subconscious.

She hadn't seen Carl from that day to this, although there was the occasional photograph of him in the newspapers, usually escorting one beautiful woman or another. As far as she knew he had never remarried, but if he had she could only pity his second wife, as she had pitied his first.

It was after ten when she woke the next morning, just time enough for her to bath and dress before Bartholomew Jordan arrived.

'Where do you think you're going?' Derek came into the bedroom just as she was getting out of bed.

Eve felt no embarrassment, not with Derek. He was used to seeing her wandering about his flat in her nightclothes. Besides, the cotton nightgown hid a lot more than the clothes she wore on stage.

'Bart Jordan isn't seeing me in bed again,' she informed him. 'It puts me at a disadvantage.'

Derek grinned. 'I'm sure he's aware of that.'

'So am I—which is why I'm getting up.'

'The doctor will be here in a minute,' he told her. 'So perhaps you should stay in bed until after he's been.'

Her eyes became stormy. 'I told you I didn't want to see a doctor!'

He shrugged. 'I didn't call him. Bart Jordan is sending his own doctor. He telephoned shortly after nine to tell me to expect the man at half past ten.'

Eve scowled angrily. 'He has no right——' she broke off as the doorbell rang. 'If that's Bart Jordan tell him I left the country late last night and you have no idea where I've gone,' she said childishly.

Derek smiled. 'And if it's the doctor?'

'Tell him—tell him——'

The door opened and Judy stood there, a tall distinguished man of about fifty standing at her side. Eve felt daunted just looking at him, the haughty expression on his face telling her that he had never before made a house-call on such a lowly dwelling, and his eyes widening slightly as he took in her crumpled nightgown. No doubt his female clients usually wore the sheerest lingerie.

'Miss Meredith?' he asked stiltedly.

She held back her amusement with difficulty, something Derek wasn't able to do, muttering his excuses and hastily leaving the room. She could hear his muffled laughter coming from the other room, his and Judy's, which meant that if she could hear them so could this doctor.

Her head went back in challenge. She hadn't asked this arrogant man here, so why should she care what he thought? 'Yes, I'm Eve Meredith,' she confirmed coolly.

His harsh features broke into a smile as he held out his hand to her. 'Edgar Holliston.'

That charming smile came as something of a surprise to her, and she accepted his hand almost dazedly.

'Bart Jordan asked me to call.' His voice was warm now.

'I—Yes. But I don't need a doctor,' she told him hurriedly. 'I——'

'Bart has already told me of your near collapse last night, Miss Meredith,' Edgar Holliston frowned. 'And if you don't mind my saying so, you sound desperately in need of a doctor.'

She did mind him saying so. Her weakness last night had been nothing, it had passed now, and she didn't appreciate this man making the incident seem more than it was.

'I'm perfectly all right now,' she insisted.

'Then it won't hurt if I just give you a little check-up, will it?' He put his black bag down on the bed, looking at her expectantly as she still stood beside the bed.

'I don't need a check-up,' she told him firmly. 'Besides, you aren't my doctor.'

'As of this morning I am.'

'This morning . . .?' Eve frowned. 'But—How?'

He shrugged. 'Bart made the arrangements for you. Now could you please lie down, Miss Meredith? I had to cancel several other appointments to come here this morning, so your co-operation would be appreciated.'

She lay down, fuming all the time he was examining her. Not that he wasn't good at his job, he was very thorough, she would just like to wring Bart Jordan's neck for him. And when he got here at eleven o'clock she just might do that!

Edgar Holliston stood back. 'Your blood pressure is slightly raised, but I would put that down to temper,' he smiled. 'Bart is only thinking of your health by insisting on these precautions,' he added gently.

Eve glared up at him. 'I've managed so far without any interference from him!'

He chuckled, and the last impression of haughtiness disappeared. 'Bart said you were a little on the fiery side,' he continued to smile.

Eve scowled. She wasn't in the least fiery, she didn't allow things to bother her enough to either enrage or anger her. And yet hadn't she been in one temper after another since her first meeting with Bart Jordan?

'I'll thank Bartholomew Jordan to keep his opinions to himself,' she said crossly.

'Back on form, I see,' he drawled from the doorway.

She turned to glare at him. 'Don't you ever knock before entering a room?' she snapped, pulling the sheet up over the open neckline of her nightgown, ever conscious that last night this man had seen her without any clothes at all.

She knew he was thinking of that too; there was a mocking quirk to his well-shaped mouth as he came farther into the room, moving with the grace of a jungle cat.

'Dr Holliston could have still been examining me,' she added in a disgruntled voice.

'I don't mind if Sir Edgar doesn't,' he taunted.

Eve looked at the doctor with accusing eyes. 'Sir Edgar?'

'Well—yes,' he looked a little bashful, 'but I rarely bother with the title.'

'How's it going, Edgar?' Bart Jordan asked briskly.

Eve shot him another resentful glance. He had no right to look so virilely healthy, not when she had the energy of a limp rag. He also had the advantage over her of being impeccably dressed, the chocolate brown trousers complemented nicely by the open-necked tan shirt. His tanned skin looked even darker, his blond hair brushed back in the casually windswept style he favoured. He looked very tall and overpowering, and Eve disliked him all the more for it.

'I've finished my examination,' Sir Edgar said thoughtfully. 'It's as you said, Bart, complete exhaustion.'

'I'm fine!' Eve instantly claimed, knowing she had never felt so tired in her life. Just the small effort of getting out of bed this morning had been almost too much for her. She felt as weak as a kitten, and she was aware that she was spitting like one when forced into a corner. But she had let a man like Bartholomew Jordan take over her life once before, she wouldn't let it happen again.

'You're far from fine,' the doctor told her sternly. 'I think perhaps I should admit you to a clinic for a week or two, make sure you get complete rest. You're a lovely young lady, Eve, but you should take more care of this body of yours. It must have been crying out for weeks now that it's had enough, that it needs to rest.'

She struggled into a sitting position, hastily doing up the buttons on her nightgown as she saw Bartholomew Jordan's green-eyed gaze lingering there. 'Maybe your body talks to you, Sir Edgar,' she scorned, 'but mine doesn't talk to me.' She ignored the memory of the occasional feelings of weakness that had been happening all too often the last few weeks. 'And I'm not going to any clinic,' she added stubbornly.

'You see what I mean?' Bart said to the doctor. 'Impossible, isn't she?'

'I——'

Sir Edgar chuckled at her look of outrage, talking to Bart. 'You would be exactly the same in Eve's position. I think you're the worst patient I've ever had for carrying out my instructions.'

Eve gave a satisfied smile, grinning even more as

Bart scowled at her. But his next comment soon wiped the smile off her face.

'If Eve refuses to go to a clinic,' he drawled, 'then I'll just have to take care of her body—the resting of it, I mean,' he added mockingly as she blushed fiery red.

Sir Edgar laughed outright now, packing his things away in his bag. 'As long as she rests,' he sobered, 'I don't care how it's achieved. And you, young lady,' he spoke sternly to Eve, 'you can do as you're told.'

'I can take care of myself,' she said defiantly.

The doctor sighed. 'Bart——'

'Don't worry,' the other man assured him, 'I'll take care of it.'

'You——'

'Eve . . . shut up,' he ordered calmly.

'I will not!' she gasped. 'And you won't take care of anything. You——' her words were cut off by the firmness of his lips being placed over hers.

She was too stunned for several minutes to do anything about it, then she began to struggle, pushing at his chest, but somehow her fingers just seemed to become entangled in the silky dark blond hair that grew there.

Bart's eyes were triumphant as he was the one to break the kiss, and Eve was speechless as he put her firmly back on the pillows. 'I shall have to remember that,' he taunted. 'Every time you talk too much I shall kiss you.'

She suddenly came out of her daze. 'You will——'

'Challenging me already, Eve?' he mocked, moving threateningly towards her.

'No!' She shrank back on to the bed.

A momentary look of puzzled irritation marked his handsome features before it was quickly masked, and his expression was bland as he turned to the doctor.

'I'll walk down to your car with you,' he offered.

'Fine.' Sir Edgar closed his bag with a snap. 'And I want my instructions carried out, Eve, or the next time I see you it could be in a hospital bed.'

She managed a jerky smile. 'I—I appreciate your help, Sir Edgar.'

'But not mine,' Bart muttered. 'Stay there until I come back,' he ordered before leaving the room with the doctor.

God, she thought, he was a bossy, autocratic, pigheaded, sarcastic——

'If looks could kill!' Derek commented with amusement.

Eve flushed, looking up at him. 'I didn't hear you come in.'

'That was obvious,' he grinned, sitting down on the bedroom chair.

'He's damned arrogant!' she said fiercely.

'I'm no more happy about the situation than you are,' he gave a rueful smile. 'But I have to agree with the man. You certainly can't go on in your condition.'

Eve gave him a sharp look. 'Can't go on . . .?' she repeated suspiciously.

'Mm,' Derek nodded. 'Of course it hasn't been easy, but then cancelling a show never is, so they tell me.' He ran a tired hand around the back of his neck, rubbing his nape wearily.

Eve gasped, her face very white. 'Are you telling me you've cancelled my show for tonight?' she was incredulous.

He frowned. '*I* haven't. Bartholomew Jordan has.'

CHAPTER FOUR

IN that moment Eve knew a rage stronger than any she had ever known before. Carl had been domineering, but even he had asked her opinion when it came to major decisions in their relationship. No one had ever dared make such an important choice for her before.

Derek backed away in mock fear. 'Don't explode, Eve,' he warned in alarm. 'You know you couldn't do a two-hour show tonight. You look as if a puff of wind would blow you away. I should have realised sooner,' he shook his head.

She was so angry she couldn't speak, her blood seeming to boil, her hands clenched into fists at her sides.

'Eve——'

'Would you leave me, Derek?' she requested through gritted teeth, staring rigidly up at the ceiling. 'I'd like to be alone for a minute.' Before she actually did someone some physical damage!

He touched her arm. 'Hey, Eve——'

'Please, Derek!' She turned fierce blue eyes on him. 'Just leave me. It isn't your fault, I realise that, but if you don't get out of here I'm going to say something I'll regret. Please, Derek,' she repeated.

'Okay,' he sighed; he had obviously never seen her like this before.

'And, Derek,' she stopped him as he reached the door, 'when Mr Bartholomew Jordan gets back I want to see him.'

'I doubt I'd be able to stop him,' he said ruefully.

'Don't even try,' she advised grimly. 'It's time

someone told him exactly what they think of him—and I'm about to do it!'

Derek grinned. 'I'll stay well clear, then!'

Eve frowned. 'Is there any chance that we can *un*-cancel tonight?'

'No. And even if there were I wouldn't do it. I've been pushing you too hard, and it's time I stopped. Just take things easy from now on, okay?'

As soon as he had left the room she got out of bed and dressed in tight-fitting brown corduroys and a pale blue tee-shirt, just managing to run her brush through her hair before she heard the even tenor of Bart Jordan's voice in the next room. She had been at a distinct disadvantage lying in bed, but now she could face him on an equal footing, or as equal as she could be when he was at least a foot taller than she was, and when she still felt so weak. The act of dressing seemed to have drained what little strength she had left.

Nevertheless, she faced Bart Jordan challengingly as he entered the room, his eyes narrowing as he saw she was out of bed and dressed.

'I thought I told you to stay in bed.'

Colour brightened her cheeks. 'No one tells me what to do, *Mr Jordan*,' she bit out furiously. 'And that includes interference in the way I run my life. How dare you cancel my show for tonight?'

'Eve——'

His patient tone angered her even more. 'Who gave you the right to just walk in and take over my life?'

'Eve——'

'Because I certainly didn't!' she continued angrily. 'You——'

'I warned you,' he said softly before giving her a gentle shove that easily knocked her down on to the bed, then quickly joining her, his body pinning her down as he held her arms above her head, her nails clenched into talons.

Eve breathed up at him, his face only inches from hers as her eyes spat her hatred of him. 'Take your hands off me!' she told him through gritted teeth.

'Now that I've got you here?' he taunted, shaking his head. 'No way am I going to let you go.' His head lowered and his mouth claimed hers.

Her nails curved to dig into the leathery skin of his hand. But the pain she knew she must be inflicting only made him all the more determined, forcing her lips apart to deepen the kiss, his body even heavier above her.

His eyes glittered deeply green as he lifted his head. 'Little wildcat, aren't you,' he said with amusement, looking at the deep indents she had made in his hand with her nails.

Eve recoiled as if he had struck her. Carl had called her that after she had scratched his back. Did all men like to give and receive pain?

Bart frowned, his hand curving about her cheek as he forced her to look at him. 'What's the matter?' he asked slowly. 'Eve, what's wrong?'

She easily pushed him off her now as he offered no resistance, and stood up to glare down at him. 'You just kissed me against my will—and not for the first time either!—and you have the nerve to ask me what's wrong? I dislike being forced, Mr Jordan, that's what's wrong!'

He slowly swung his legs to the floor, sitting up, very lithe and attractive in the casual clothing. He stood up to move to the door.

Eve frowned. 'Where are you going?' She hadn't expected her outburst to make him leave! She was far from finished yet.

He turned hard green eyes on her. 'Do you care?' he rasped, his face suddenly bleak.

'Well, I——'

'I'll be back.' His mouth twisted. 'Don't worry, I'm not leaving.'

'I'm not worried,' she snapped. 'In fact, I would be glad if you did leave.'

'I know that,' he taunted. 'But I have no intention of doing so. We have things to discuss.'

'Things?' she echoed sharply. 'What sort of things?'

'Patience, Eve,' he mocked. 'It's supposed to be a virtue, you know.'

'How would you know, you don't have any!'

To her chagrin he smiled. 'Where's the sophisticated woman of our first meeting?' he taunted. 'You're acting like a child. All this resentment because I had the good sense to tell Derek you weren't going to do your show tonight.'

She flushed, knowing he was right about the childish behaviour. 'I like to make those sort of decisions for myself,' she defended.

He sighed. 'But would you?'

Her lips came together firmly. 'I don't know, do I?' she answered resentfully. 'I didn't get the choice.'

Bart shook his head. 'Derek's already told me you wanted to go on with it, so don't pretend you would have decided otherwise. Maybe I should have let you go on,' he added harshly. 'Maybe you deserve to have a nervous breakdown and land up in hospital, as Edgar said you would. Is that what you want, Eve?' He was angry too now, once again the autocratic stranger of their first meeting. It wasn't until he reverted to being that man that she realised how teasingly he had been behaving with her. It seemed strange to think of the hated Bartholomew Jordan in a gentle mood. 'Is it?' he demanded roughly.

She looked down at her feet. 'You know it isn't,' she mumbled.

'Then stop acting like a spoilt child, and start enjoying the narrow escape you've had!' The force with which he slammed the door told her how deep his anger was.

He was right, she knew he was right, she just wished he hadn't been the one to make the decision. It made her feel as if the control of her life was slipping out of her hands, and since Carl she had grown fiercely independent, valuing that independence above everything else.

Bart was back within minutes, partly obscured by the hugest bouquet of mixed flowers she had ever seen. She had thought the dozens of roses to be big, but this—this was immense!

He grinned as he lowered the flowers, looking curiously younger than the thirty-nine years he claimed to be. 'There must be *one* among these that you do like,' he smiled, holding them out to her.

Tears filled her eyes and she blinked them back hastily. She never cried, never! It must be the weakness she was feeling, it couldn't be because of the flowers Bart had bought her.

'And there's these,' he produced a massive box of chocolates, 'to help fatten you up.'

Her mouth twitched and finally she smiled, a clear untroubled smile that made Bart's eyes widen in appreciation. 'Thank you,' she said huskily. 'I—I don't deserve them.'

'No, you don't,' he instantly agreed.

She spluttered with laughter, and sat down weakly on the bed. 'You're very blunt.'

Bart nodded. 'About as blunt as you are. And I like that, it isn't something you find very often in a woman nowadays.'

He would have had plenty of women in his life, Eve knew that. Hadn't he admitted to having a mistress at this very moment? He was a very handsome man, he probably had to fight the women off. Then why was he bothering with her? The answer to that seemed all too obvious. He was a man who would enjoy a challenge, and at the moment she presented one.

She shrugged dismissively. 'Maybe you've just been meeting the wrong women, Mr Jordan.'

'Maybe,' he agreed huskily, putting the chocolates down on the bed beside her. 'But I've met you now. And I wish you would call me Bart, it's much more friendly.'

Precisely the reason she wouldn't call him it! 'Mr Jordan——'

'I can assure you I have no intention of calling you Miss Meredith,' he added persuasively.

'So I've noticed,' she said dryly. 'You said we had things to discuss, Mr Jordan. Would you mind telling me what they are?'

He leant back casually against the wardrobe, easily the most dangerously attractive man she had ever met. Even more attractive than Carl, more ruggedly so; the lines of cynicism beside his mouth had been put there by experience and not by cruelty.

But she shouldn't be noticing how handsome he was, or comparing him with Carl! Especially as Bartholomew Jordan seemed to be coming out more favourably in the comparison! He was made from the same mould, she refused to believe otherwise.

'Well?' she prompted tautly, her thoughts disturbing her.

His gaze was warm on her angrily flushed features. 'Have you always worn your hair loose?'

A hand instantly went up selfconsciously to touch her long dark tresses. 'Not always, no,' she replied awkwardly, frowning.

'I like it.'

She gave an impatient sigh. 'I'm sure my hair wasn't one of the things you wanted to discuss,' she snapped.

'Oh, but it was,' he said deeply. 'Also those deep blue pools you have for eyes, your beautiful long dark lashes, that pert little nose that at this moment is going higher and higher in your indignation, and lastly your mouth.' His voice lowered huskily. 'Your mouth is beautiful, Eve. Every time I look at it I want to kiss it, to——'

'Do you mind!' she cut in furiously, her cheeks burning from the way his gaze had been hungrily fixed on her mouth.

'I don't mind at all,' he drawled mockingly. 'You're the most exciting woman I've ever met, both visually and mentally.'

She stood up, her movements agitated. 'Stop talking to me like that! Perhaps we should join Derek and Judy in the other room.' She felt too isolated with him here, too vulnerable, even though she knew the other couple were only in the other room.

Bart sighed. 'Okay, Eve, I'll stop telling you how beautiful and attractive I find you. You obviously don't want to hear it.'

'No,' she confirmed abruptly, distrusting the things he had told her. Carl had told her things just as complimentary, and all the time he had a wife. Bart might not be married, but she felt sure his words were just as insincere.

'Then we'll get down to business,' he said briskly.

She gave him a sharp look, searching his hard features. 'What business?' she asked suspiciously.

'The business of getting you to rest.'

'Surely that is *my* business?' she told him pointedly.

'It should be,' he nodded. 'But you don't seem to care how you abuse your body——'

'Abuse?' she repeated tautly, a dark flush colouring her cheeks. 'I don't abuse my body, Mr Jordan. I don't need to—I can leave that to men like you.'

His jaw tightened, his eyes suddenly an icy green. 'You call a few kisses "abuse"——'

Eve nodded. 'If they're against my will, yes.'

He drew in an angry breath, suddenly tense. 'Okay,' he said tightly, 'I won't kiss you again unless you ask me to.'

'And that will never happen!'

'Let's wait and see, shall we?'

'As I never intend to see you again after today I don't think we should "wait and see" at all,' she told him with saccharine sweetness.

'You'll be seeing me, Eve,' he informed her. 'Almost every day for the next month or so.'

She gasped. 'What do you mean?'

'Edgar said you were to rest, and I mean to make sure that you do. I have a house in Hampshire, you're going to stay there for at least a month——'

'I am not!'

'At least a month,' he repeated firmly. 'During which time you will do nothing but relax and let my housekeeper put some flesh back on your bones.'

'You really think that I'll just let you walk in here and start ordering my life about?' she scorned, taken aback by this man's arrogance. She shook her head. 'Because if you do you don't know me very well, Mr Jordan.'

'I don't know you at all,' he admitted softly. 'But I'm trying my damnedest to.'

'Well, you won't do it this way!' she snapped. 'God, I've met some arrogant men in my time—too many of them, but I think you take first prize. I don't even know you, and what I do know I don't particularly like, and yet you calmly expect me to become a guest

in your home for a month.' She shook her head
dazedly. 'I think you must be insane, Mr Jordan!'

He seemed to be having difficulty controlling his
own anger. 'I'll admit,' he finally said tautly, 'that I
may have gone about things the wrong way with you,
you obviously react better to persuasion than you do
to coercion.'

'I don't *react* well to either of those things, I like to
make my own decisions.'

'Then make one now!' he rasped. 'You need rest,
looking after——'

'Which I can get quite adequately in my own home.'

'No,' he shook his head. 'You live alone——'

'I live with my godparents.'

'You live on a houseboat at the end of their property
on the Norfolk Broads. And they aren't even there at
the moment, they're working on some archaeological
expedition in Egypt.'

'How do you know all this?' she gasped.

'I made it my business to know,' he told her grimly.
'I also know that you have no near neighbours, that
you have to walk two miles to the nearest shop, that
you have to carry buckets of water from your godparents' house to fill up your own water supply,
that——'

'You seem to have done your homework well, Mr
Jordan. Derek?' she queried bitterly.

'He and I discussed where you should go to rest——'

'Without asking me?' she exploded. 'God, you have
a nerve, both of you! I'll go where I damn well please,
and nothing you or Derek say will make the slightest
bit of difference.'

'Are you intent on killing yourself?' Bart demanded
angrily. 'Can't you see we're only trying to do what's
best for you?'

'What's best for you, you mean! I take it that after

I'd rested all day, been fattened up by your house-keeper, my nights would be spent a little more strenu-ously?' Her mouth twisted bitterly. 'That I would be expected to keep the master of the house's bed warm—namely you?'

Derek opened the door, a worried frown on his face; he had obviously heard the raised voices. 'Is everything all right?'

Bart Jordan's fierce gaze never left Eve's scornful face. 'Get out!' he thundered at the other man. 'And don't come back unless I ask you to!'

'But——'

Cold green eyes were turned on him sharply. 'I said get out, Derek,' Bart ordered in a chilling voice.

Eve didn't like the dangerous glitter in his eyes. In this mood Bart Jordan frightened her, and she realised that she had been the one to cause his anger.

Derek gave a resigned shrug, then slowly moved back out of the room and closed the door behind him.

Bart Jordan moved forward to grasp Eve's arms painfully in his hands, glaring down at her. 'I think you've done enough talking for one day,' he told her in a harsh voice. 'Now it's time you listened. You're a bad-tempered shrew, and if you were feeling stronger I would put you over my knee and give you the hiding you deserve!'

'You and whose army?' she taunted.

'Don't tempt me, Eve,' he ground out. 'Right now it would give me great pleasure to tan your backside. But I'm not going to, you ungrateful little wildcat.' He seemed not to care as once again she flinched at his use of that name for her. 'I won't give you the pleasure of having another excuse to dislike me.'

Her eyes flashed deeply blue. 'I don't need an excuse—I can't bear you near me!'

'You're so full of self-pity you can't——'

'Self-pity?' she repeated shrilly.

'Some man hurt you, and now you think every other man you meet is going to do the same,' he scowled darkly. 'Well, here's one man who isn't going to continue battering his head against a brick wall!' He walked angrily to the door. 'I've tried to help you, Miss Meredith, but some people just don't want to be helped. Run yourself into the ground, half kill yourself—why the hell should I care!' He slammed the door on his way out.

Eve dropped down heavily on to the bed. Well, she had done it now, that should get Bart Jordan out of her life once and for all.

Derek came in a few minutes later, a curiously pale Derek. 'What the hell have you been saying to the man?' he demanded.

She looked up at him with full eyes, the weakness back now that her argument with Bart Jordan was over. 'Just the truth,' she sighed.

'And his offer to take care of you for a while?'

'I told him exactly what he could do with it!'

'Oh, Eve, Eve!' He shook his head. 'What have you done now?'

Life sparkled in her eyes once more. 'I've stopped his interference once and for all. You have no right to discuss my private life with him, Derek, no right at all. You told him all about my godparents, and where I live. I don't like your having done that, especially to him.'

His blue eyes narrowed. 'You keep saying that, but why him especially?'

'Because—because——'

'Can it be that you really like him but that you're afraid to admit it, even to yourself?'

'No, it can't!' she snapped. 'I hate him!'

Derek shrugged, sighing. 'If you say so. But now

what are we going to do about getting you rested? You could stay here, I suppose——'

'I'm going home.'

'To the houseboat?' he frowned.

'Yes.'

'That's damned stupid, Eve, and you know it,' he scowled. 'There's no way I'm going to let you go back there while you're in this state.'

'There's no way you're going to stop me,' she told him calmly. 'And I'm just a little tired, not in a "state". A couple of days' rest and I'll be fine.'

'That isn't what the doctor said.'

She shrugged. 'He's used to dealing with the idle rich, Derek. They probably enjoy being told to rest for a month. We lesser mortals don't have time for it.' She gave him a searching look. 'How is all this going to affect my career?'

He looked away, his expression suddenly guarded. 'Too soon to tell,' he murmured. 'The important thing now is to get you well.'

'Derek?' she probed softly. 'The truth, now.'

He shrugged. 'Like I said, it's too soon to tell.'

'But . . .?'

He sighed. 'Let's just say maybe I should start scouting around for a new star.'

Eve bit her lip. 'As bad as that?'

'I just don't know. You said you wanted the truth?'

'Yes,' she nodded.

'Well then, it could be that bad.' He sat down next to her, his arm about her shoulders. 'You don't really have it in you, do you?' he probed gently. 'Oh, you can sing, but then so can hundreds of other girls. Bart Jordan made me realise that it was only my pushing that had got you this far, that you don't really have the drive to make it to the top.'

Her face coloured angrily. 'And just when did he convince you of that?'

'Last night.' He grimaced. 'I should have realised before. You were reluctant to commit yourself to doing these concerts, when most girls would sell their soul for a chance like that. You know it's the truth, Eve. Don't let your dislike of Bart Jordan make you say any differently.'

'Derek——'

'Eve, be honest with yourself if not with me.'

She sighed. 'Okay, so maybe I've realised my reluctance too. But where does that leave me?'

He shrugged. 'Where do you want it to leave you?'

She looked down at her hands. 'You really want to know?'

He nodded. 'I really do.'

She took a deep breath, searching for the right words. Derek had been a good friend to her over the last five years, had moulded her career, had given her the minor success she had today.

'It's all right, Eve,' he gave a rueful grin, 'I think I know what you want. You want to go back to Norfolk and never have to face an audience again, right?'

'Yes,' she admitted huskily, looking at him pleadingly for understanding. 'I'm really grateful for what you've done for me, and I've enjoyed—most of it. But——'

'It's the "buts" of this world that usually mean trouble,' he derided.

'I'm sorry, Derek, I really am. I just don't think I'm cut out for this type of life. I've tried, but I—I——'

'You hate it.'

'Yes.' Oh, it was a relief just to be able to admit it, to say the words out loud.

'I already guessed that.' He shrugged. 'So we drop the idea of you becoming the next Kate Bush. You look a bit like her, you know. You have that same air of mystery about you. Of course, you're more beautiful, but——'

'Flattery, Derek? From you?' she mocked gently.

'From me,' he nodded, smiling. 'You have a terrific voice, Eve, husky and sexy. Your body is beautiful, and you have the face of an angel, but if your heart isn't in what we're trying to achieve then we may as well forget it.'

She knew he was right, had known it for some time but had been too afraid to admit it. And she hadn't wanted to let Derek down, had known the lengths he had gone to to get her the few breaks she had had. For every girl who succeeded in this business there were thousands who never made it out of the second-rate clubs she used to sing in.

As Derek said, she had a voice, a reasonably attractive face, but she couldn't live up to the image she had created. It was time to drop out and give one of those other girls a chance.

'What will happen about tonight?' she asked. 'We'll lose money on it, and——'

'It's all been taken care of,' Derek dismissed.

'The backers——'

'Backer—in the singular,' he corrected.

Her eyes opened wide with alarm. 'Oh, my God, not——'

'Yes,' Derek sighed heavily, 'Bart Jordan financed the whole thing.'

She was very pale. 'But you told me——' she frowned, swallowing hard. 'I know for a fact that we had four or five backers to start with.'

'Yes, but Bart Jordan approached me several months ago and offered to pay for it all. It seemed too good an opportunity to miss at the time.' He groaned. 'I wish to God I'd never started it!'

So did she. It put her under a liability to Bartholomew Jordan. No wonder he thought he had the right to dictate to her whether or not she did the show tonight! It also made her wonder whether she could have misunderstood his interest of the last few nights. He could have just been at the shows to keep an eye on his investment.

'How much money is he losing?' she asked, dreading the answer.

Derek shrugged. 'Who knows? He's been dealing with the financial side of things. I think we just about broke even the last four nights, so I suppose he lost all of tonight's takings, plus the musicians still have to be paid. The theatre was booked for five nights too. He'll be out a few thousand, I suppose. Not that he can't afford it, but——'

'But that isn't the point,' she finished grimly. 'Oh God,' she groaned, 'I've never owed anyone money in my life, and now it seems I owe Bart Jordan thousands!'

'Don't be silly, Eve.' Derek patted her hand. 'You don't owe him anything. This was an investment for him, just like any other business deal he might make. He knew the odds when he made the offer.'

She frowned. 'And you say he approached you?'

'Mm,' he nodded.

'What did he say, his exact words?'

'I can't remember that, love,' Derek laughed dismissively. 'I was smashed at the time. Judy and I were at some party or other—you know the sort I mean, too much booze and no food.'

She grimaced. 'Too much free sex too.' She had been to one of Derek's 'scouting' parties, as he called them, and after the sixth approach, obviously sexual ones, she had left.

'That too,' he acknowledged. 'It was a bad night for me. One of the backers had just dropped out and I was having trouble getting a replacement. Bart Jordan's offer was like a gift from heaven. But he insisted he be the only one involved in the deal.'

Eve gave him a sharp look. 'Deal? What deal?'

He licked his lips, obviously nervous, something unusual for him. 'I agreed to let him have your contract if things didn't work out,' he revealed reluctantly.

'You——! Derek, you can't do that without consulting me, surely?' she gasped.

He looked sheepish. 'I didn't think you would ever need to know about it. I was so sure you were going to make it.'

'What happens now?' she asked dully. 'Do I belong to Bartholomew Jordan?'

'*You* don't belong to anyone, your career does.'

'To Bart Jordan.'

Derek gave her a reproachful look. 'He isn't the devil himself, Eve.'

'Isn't he?'

'Eve!'

'Okay, I'm sorry.' She put a hand up to her aching temple, sighing deeply. 'He didn't get such a bargain, anyway. I'm not going to sing publicly again.'

'And you aren't going to fight the fact that he now has your contract?' Derek seemed surprised by her lack of fight.

'Why should I?' she shrugged. 'He can't make me work. That contract just entitles him to fifteen per cent of whatever I earn. In future that will be nil.'

'Eve,' Derek put his hand on her arm, 'I really didn't think it would come to this. I've really landed you in it, haven't I?'

She shook her head, her smile wan. 'I landed myself in it. I should have been honest with you from the start.'

'And I shouldn't have pushed you so damned hard.

I'm responsible for the exhaustion you're suffering.'

'No,' she assured him, 'there were faults on both sides. And my only consolation is that my contract runs out in six months' time. Maybe I can stay out of Bart Jordan's way for that amount of time.'

'The way he walked out of here I doubt you'll see him again,' Derek grinned.

'I hope not.' She frowned. '*Can* he make me work, Derek?'

'Not if you don't want to. You know our contract was only drawn up in the first place for business reasons, it never meant a damn thing, and it has so many loopholes . . .' He shrugged. 'I think that's why I let him have it.'

She doubted Bart Jordan regarded the contract in such a casual light. After all, why agree to take it if he didn't intend using it? But maybe once she was back in Norfolk she would never see him again. Derek seemed to think that was what would happen. She certainly hoped so.

Derek and Judy were against her going back to Norfolk, voicing their objections right up to the time she got on the train. When it had become clear that she was adamant about going Derek had offered to drive her, an offer she had declined. Derek was used to driving in London traffic, and his driving certainly wasn't conducive to rest and relaxation. At least on the train she could go to sleep if she wanted to, without fear of hitting something or someone while she slept.

Norfolk and her home were everything she remembered them being—and they were a lot more besides! All the drawbacks Bart Jordan had pointed out to her turned out to be reality.

She loved this part of England, the stark flatness that had a beauty of its own. The Broads were beautiful this time of year, all the mother ducks proudly showing off their young, the little soft downy creatures following as their mothers swam majestically down the river. Eve could sit and view this scene from her houseboat actually on the Broads, but sometimes she would take her rowboat out to Salhouse Broad to see the many families of migratory geese that nested in the sandy-shored inlet there.

But not this year. Right now she was having trouble just surviving. The water buckets had never seemed so heavy, or the walk to the shop so far. Not that she had any appetite for the food she bought, but as she had to make the walk anyway to telephone Derek from the callbox there she bought some supplies at the same time. It would save her the trouble of having to make the journey again when she did feel like eating.

She realised after walking the first mile back down the rough track to the houseboat that she had overdone the shopping; the last mile was just pure torture to her. By the time she reached her home it was all she could do to stagger down the steps and collapse on to the couch in the living area. So much for reassuring Derek that she was well, and able to take care of herself!

Right now she just wished that Aunt Sophy and Uncle George were back from Egypt. Her uncle had been an archaeologist for as long as she could remember, and Aunt Sophy always went with him on his trips, Eve too when she was younger. She wished now that she had gone with them this time.

Aunt Sophy disapproved of her career as a singer, she also disapproved of the houseboat Eve had insisted on living on as soon as she was old enough to have her own home. This way she managed to have her privacy and a family at the same time. Not that Aunt Sophy and Uncle George were really family, but they had cared for her since she was twelve years old, taking their responsibility as her godparents very seriously.

Oh, how she wished they were here now, Aunt Sophy fussing over her, Uncle George quietly vague as he always was. But they weren't here, and she was too tired to move from the couch, her last thought before she fell asleep that the frozen food still in the shopping bag would all go off if she didn't get it into her tiny freezer.

When she woke up it was four o'clock in the morning. She had slept for twelve hours!

Not that she felt any better for it; her movements were weary as she struggled to sit up, licking her dry lips. She was very thirsty, cold too, the tee-shirt she had been wearing that afternoon was no barrier against the coldness of the Norfolk nights. She rubbed her chilled arms, pulling a thick sweater out of a cupboard before moving to the stove to make herself a warming cup of tea.

Damn, damn, damn! The gas cylinder was empty. She would have to go outside and change the valve over to her spare tank. These cylinders usually lasted a few weeks, and she remembered now that it was almost a month since she had replaced it.

It was even colder outside, a fine summer rain was falling from the darkened sky, and her feet slipped on the damp grass as she walked around to the back of the houseboat, her canvas shoes getting soaked in the process.

She reached out to pull herself on to the back of the houseboat, and her feet somehow slipped from beneath her. She had no time to do anything, no way of stopping herself as she fell with a loud splash into the murky, dark water.

The Norfolk Broads were known for the fierceness of their currents, fatalities occurring every year, both holidaymakers and local fishermen alike. But there was no fear of that in this quiet inlet of water that belonged to her aunt and uncle, being a way for them to manoeuvre their motor-cruiser out on to the main Broad.

But her lack of strength was making it difficult for her to get up on to the muddy bank. She grabbed handfuls of grass, cutting her hands on its sharp edges as she kept slipping back into the water, and each time it was becoming more of a struggle to reach the side and try again. The water looked so deep and inviting, almost warm and comforting, it's arms seeming to reach out to her and draw her downwards, ever downwards.

And then she thought of Bart Jordan's 'I told you so' look when she told him she was dead. She was so tired and confused that the illogicality of such a thought didn't even occur to her. All she knew was that it was the added incentive she needed to drag herself up on to the muddy bank and into the long wet grass.

But that was as far as that burst of energy would take her; she dropped face down into the grass, her hair matted with water and mud combined, her clothes and face equally dirty, her hands cut and bleeding.

Suddenly it wasn't just dark any more, it was pitch black, a curious feeling of peace washing over her as she slipped quietly into oblivion.

CHAPTER FIVE

IF only she could open her eyes—but her lids felt as if they were glued together, or maybe they were just too heavy for her to lift. And she couldn't move, she felt— she felt paralysed.

She groaned, more of a whimper really. At once the light she could detect through her closed lids was blacked out.

'Eve?' a huskily male voice was prompting. 'Eve, are you in pain?'

How could she be in pain when she couldn't feel anything? And who was this man? His voice sounded familiar, but——

'Eve?' his voice sharpened with concern. 'Shall I get someone to help you?'

Someone to help her? Who? She was alone, so completely alone. She remembered now, remembered falling, the shock of the cold water, dragging herself back on to the bank. This man must be an hallucination. She was alone, no one would even think of checking on her until she missed Derek's call on Saturday. Yes, this man was an hallucination, and one didn't talk to an hallucination.

'Eve, for God's sake!' the voice rasped. 'I know you can hear me, you just smiled. Eve, for God's sake open your eyes!'

She frowned. She did know that voice, it belonged to Bart Jordan. God, if she was going to hallucinate why couldn't it be about someone she liked!

'Open your eyes, damn you!' he ordered sharply.

'Don't you swear at me,' she said in a choked rasping

voice. 'This is my hallucination,' her bottom lip quivered emotionally. 'The least you could do is be nice to me.' Tears squeezed out below her heavy lids.

She heard a muttered curse, and then, wonder of wonders, arms came about her, warm protective arms, not beckoning and enticing like the cold water, but solid human arms that sought to give comfort.

'Eve,' his voice was next to her ear now, his breath stirring her hair, 'if you'll just open your eyes, darling, you'll see I'm very real.'

She swallowed hard, afraid to do as he asked, terrified of losing him, of being alone again. But the arms felt real, painfully so as they tightened about her frail body. Her lids fluttered open with effort, and she looked straight up into deep green eyes, the lamplight behind Bart showing him big and strong, the darkness outside surrounding them like a cloak.

'Bart . . .' she croaked.

He gave a tight smile, a pulse working erratically at his jawline. 'God, Eve,' he breathed huskily, 'you've had me worried out of my mind!'

She frowned. 'I—I have?' Each word was an effort, her throat very dry.

His arms tightened. 'When I saw you—when I found you—Oh God, I thought you were dead!' His lips feverishly caressed her brow.

Her dry lips curved into a wan smile. 'Did you think you'd lost your investment?' She had tried to tease, to ease the strain he appeared to be under, but somehow the words came out all wrong, and Bart's face darkened with anger.

'It's in your favour that I know how weak you are,' he snapped, scowling heavily, 'or else I'd put you over my knee and give you the hiding you deserve for that remark.'

'That's the second time you've threatened me,' she

recalled softly, glad that he still held her.

He nodded impatiently. 'The third time I may find you strong enough to take your punishment.'

She frowned. 'You wouldn't really hit me?'

'No,' he sighed as she seemed to flinch. 'Much as I know it would give you pleasure to think it, beating women has never been one of my faults. I have plenty of others—which I'm sure you'll be only too happy to tell me about once you're well again.'

She licked her lips. 'I—Could I have a drink, please?'

'Of course, how stupid of me.' His arms dropped away and he moved to the jug that stood on the side table. 'Iced water,' he told her, helping her sit up and drink some of the refreshing liquid.

Eve lay back with a sigh, looking up trustingly at him. 'Thank you.'

Bart smiled. 'I think I like you all weak and helpless,' and he moved to sit on the chair beside the bed.

'No!' She looked up at him pleadingly. 'Sit here,' she patted the bed beside her.

He frowned. 'Eve——'

'Oh, please, Bart.' Tears flooded her eyes. 'I was alone for so long. I—I thought I was going to die—alone. I need you to hold me——' Her voice broke emotionally as she turned away, hating having to beg. 'It was so dark,' she recalled in a tortured voice. 'The water was so cold, and—and yet inviting.' She turned bright blue eyes on him. 'I thought of giving in to its beckoning,' she admitted chokingly, knowing she had to talk about it or dam it up in the back of her mind like some guilty secret.

'God, no!' Bart pulled her roughly against the hard wall of his chest, his face now grey beneath his tan. 'Not you, Eve,' he shook his head. 'I don't believe it.'

'Yes,' she insisted softly.

His arms tightened, his cheek resting on the top of her head. 'What stopped you?'

'I—Oh, I don't know.' She moved her shoulders helplessly, knowing *he* was the reason she hadn't died, her dislike of him. But she didn't dislike him any more—how could she? She owed him her life twice over, once for giving her the will to crawl out of the water, and once for finding her before she died of the wet and the cold. She couldn't dislike him, she owed him too much.

'Eve?' he prompted huskily.

She burrowed against his chest. 'Tell me how you came to find me. Why did you go to the houseboat?'

'I'm not sure I should tell you anything,' he said sternly. 'This is a hospital, you know, and I think we may have talked too long already.'

Eve frowned, looking around the room with new eyes. It didn't look like a hospital room, it looked like a bedroom in a house, although it wasn't usual to have a television in a bedroom, not in the houses she knew anyway.

She looked up at Bart. 'Have I been very ill?'

He nodded, absently smoothing the hair at her temple. 'You still are. The doctors only just stopped the infection on your chest from turning to pneumonia.'

'Oh,' she gulped.

'Mm,' he agreed grimly. 'You've been here a week now, and listening to you trying to breathe ...' he shook his head. 'It was pure agony,' he groaned.

'You've been here a lot?'

'Quite a bit. We still haven't been able to contact your godparents.'

'Derek?' she probed.

'He's been here every day as well, Judy too. We've taken it in turns to sit with you. Which reminds me, I'd better let the doctor know you're awake.'

She grasped his hand as he would have moved away, gaining strength just from touching him. 'You aren't going to leave me?' she said desperately.

Bart looked down at her with brooding eyes, his gaze passing down to where she had entwined her fingers with his. 'You don't want me to?' he questioned huskily.

'No.'

'Then I won't,' he smiled gently. 'But you'll have to let go,' he held up their joined hands. 'I have to ring for the nurse,' he explained.

Colour flooded her cheeks, made even more noticeable against the paleness of her cheeks. 'I'm sorry,' she released his hand, 'I—I didn't mean to cling.' She turned her face into the pillow, biting her bottom lip to stop the tears from flowing. She felt so weak, so helpless, this man the only solid thing in her world at the moment.

Gentle fingers came under her chin to turn her to face him. 'Cling all you want Eve,' Bart told her. 'After what you must have gone through you have the right.'

Her bottom lip trembled precariously. 'No reprimands? No "I told you so's"?'

'Not yet. But later,' he added grimly.

She had thought he was letting her off lightly. Once she was well she felt sure she would know the full extent of his displeasure. And strangely she didn't resent his presence in her life any more, her dislike had evaporated. In its place she felt relief at being alive, and also—also she found herself liking the casual elegance with which Bart wore his cream trousers and dark green shirt, liked the way the shirt showed off his powerful shoulders and flat tapered waistline, the way the trousers moulded to his slim hips and muscular thighs. For the first time she was noticing—and appreciating—how handsome Bart was.

Carl was a thing of the past, and Bart was proving all the time that he was nothing like him. Carl wouldn't have wasted time sitting with her, the one time she had had a cold he had told her to call him once she was well again—at his office, of course, never at his home.

Bart turned from ringing for the nurse, frowning as he saw she was watching him. 'What are you thinking?' he demanded to know.

She smiled. 'You still haven't told me why you were at the houseboat,' she reminded him, not willing to disclose her thoughts to this man, not yet. Her barriers weren't down enough for that.

'That's because the question doesn't really need an answer. I was looking for you, of course.' He moved back to sit on the side of the bed.

She quirked a teasing eyebrow. 'After telling me you didn't care if I killed myself?'

Instead of the answering smile she had been expecting he scowled heavily. 'I didn't expect you to take me literally!'

'Oh, Bart——'

A young nurse quietly opened the door. 'You rang, Mr—Miss Meredith!' Her face brightened. 'You're awake!'

Eve returned the girl's smile. 'Yes.'

The nurse nodded. 'I'll just let the doctor know.' She left the room as quietly as she had entered.

Eve frowned. 'Just where am I?' The thought had suddenly occurred to her.

'Norwich,' Bart supplied.

That's what she had thought, the nurse's accent was unmistakably the Norfolk dialect. 'Then shouldn't you be in London?' she puzzled.

'I should be,' he agreed. 'But I could hardly just leave you here.'

'Oh.' Her lashes lowered to hide the sudden pain in her eyes.

'Not that I wanted to,' he teasingly knocked her chin with his fist. 'You are feeling sensitive, aren't you?'

She bit her lip. 'I suppose I am. Sorry.'

'And all this meekness isn't you either,' he mocked.

Eve looked up, her eyes flashing. 'I'm sorry if you don't like it!' she snapped.

He smiled. 'That's better. I wouldn't know you if you started being pleasant to me.'

Her expression changed to one of guilt, the fire dying from her eyes. 'I've been a bitch to you, haven't I?' she sighed.

'You have—but I'll forgive you if you promise to get better. By the way, you've become an overnight sensation,' he taunted.

Her eyes widened. 'I have?'

'Mm,' Bart nodded. 'As far as the public are concerned you seem to have disappeared off the face of the earth. Your absence is certainly making the heart grow fonder, your record has reached number twenty in the charts.'

'But it was only forty-nine last week!'

'The press seem to think you've done a Greta Garbo on them,' he grinned. 'You know "I want to be alone", so your doting public are buying what appears to be your last record.'

'It is,' she told him quietly. 'If you manoeuvred for my contract thinking you would make a lot of money from me then you're going to be out of luck. I'm never going into a recording studio again.'

A pulse beat erratically at his jaw, and he stood up. 'I didn't *manoeuvre* for your contract at all, Derek offered it as an act of good faith,' he said harshly. 'Remind me to tell you some time why I did accept it.'

Eve looked up at him, wishing she could see behind

the guarded green eyes. 'Why not now?' she queried huskily.

'Because now obviously isn't the right time,' he dismissed tersely.

'Why——'

The doctor came in at that moment, followed closely by the friendly young nurse, and asked Bart to leave so that they could examine her.

'Bart!' Eve's strangled cry stopped him at the door. He turned slowly, frowning. 'Yes?'

She licked her lips, suddenly nervous of how important he had become to her. 'You—you aren't leaving, are you?' Her eyes were unknowingly haunted.

'I——'

'Mr Jordan will have to leave in a few minutes,' the doctor interrupted firmly. 'Now that you're over the worst I think he should get some rest himself. I don't want another patient on my hands,' he added lightly.

She bit her lip guiltily, looking down at her hands. 'Of course,' she said quietly. 'I'm sorry, Bart.' She looked up, her expression deliberately guarded. 'Of course you should go and rest.'

He frowned broodingly, shooting the doctor an impatient look. 'I'll come back and see you before I go.'

'Just for a few minutes,' the doctor warned.

'I'll be back,' Bart repeated in a strong voice, his gaze reassuring on Eve. 'Perhaps we could talk when you've finished, Doctor?' His voice hardened angrily, his stance one of challenge.

Eve saw the younger man flush, and wondered how many other men would dare to talk to a doctor in such a way. Not many, she would wager. And it was all her fault!

'I'm sorry,' she told the doctor once Bart had gone outside to wait until the examination was over. 'I'm afraid Bart—Mr Jordan's anger was my fault.' She looked up anxiously.

'Not at all,' the doctor dismissed easily. 'Mr Jordan has been under great strain. We've hardly been able to pry him away from your side day or night. I would appreciate your help in getting him to go back to his hotel and sleep.'

'Of course,' she nodded eagerly, silent as he examined her. Bart had been with her day and night? But he had said he, Derek and Judy had taken it in turns to sit with her, yet the doctor certainly wasn't giving that impression. And he had called her 'darling' when she first woke up. What did it all mean?

The doctor stood back, his examination complete. 'Well, everything is in order,' he smiled. 'I expect you would like to sleep now?'

Considering that she was supposed to have been asleep for the past week she was still very tired. 'When can I have this taken away?' she indicated the needle going into her arm feeding her liquid from the plastic bag suspended above the bed.

'Now, if you like,' again he smiled.

'I like,' she accepted eagerly, finding the plastic tubing from the bag to the needle rather cumbersome.

'Nurse Evans will do that while I step outside and talk to Mr Jordan,' he said briskly.

Eve turned away as the hollow plastic needle was removed from her arm; the skin felt very tender there. 'Why did I have that?' she frowned, finding her arm felt slightly stiff.

Nurse Evans taped a dressing over the tiny puncture mark in her arm. 'You weren't taking in any fluid yourself, and so to stop you becoming dehydrated this was giving you some. Now that you're awake and can drink for yourself it's no longer necessary. You can probably eat a little tomorrow too. I'd better go now and let Mr Jordan come in and say goodnight.' She gave a conspiratorial smile. 'All the nurses on this ward have fallen for your boy-friend, Miss Meredith.'

'Oh, but he isn't——'

'No, I'm not,' Bart said from the open doorway. 'But you can thank your colleagues for me, Nurse Evans,' he added with a smile, a smile that Eve could see didn't reach his pebble-hard eyes.

The young nurse fled, an embarrassed tinge to her cheeks as she hurried out the door he held open for her.

Eve giggled. 'Now you've embarrassed her.'

There was no answering smile for her on Bart's compressed lips. 'The doctor tells me that you endorse his opinion that I should leave you now,' he said curtly.

'I—Well, I——' she frowned as she tried to remember exactly what she had said. 'I don't think those were my exact words,' she finished lamely, knowing Bart was deeply displeased by the way he still scowled at her.

'Then what the hell did you say?' He pulled the chair out next to the bed, and sat down abruptly, looking very dark in the light from the small night-light the doctor had left on.

Eve plucked nervously at the sheet. 'I think I—I agreed with him that you looked tired.'

'Then you do want me to leave?' he snapped.

'I—I—Oh, Bart!' she looked at him appealingly. 'It wasn't meant that way. But you need rest——'

He stood up forcefully. 'Then I'd better go, hadn't I? No doubt Derek and Judy will be in to see you in the morning.' He moved to the door.

'Bart!'

He turned with barely controlled anger. 'What now?'

'What now?' as if he had done enough for her, wasted

enough time, already. And hadn't he? Wasn't it solely due to him that she was even alive? And he had been in Norfolk for a week when his work and friends were in London. He was no doubt paying for this private room too. Yes, he had done enough for her already.

'Nothing.' She shook her head, falling back on the pillow, holding back her tears with difficulty. 'I suppose you'll be returning to London tomorrow?'

Bart frowned, pushing back his fair hair with impatient fingers. 'And why should you think that?' he asked slowly.

'Because I—You've been away from your—friends long enough.'

His mouth twisted. 'If you mean mistress, Eve, then say mistress. Or doesn't that word come easily to your pure little lips?'

The sneering tone had her searching his face anxiously. Why on earth was he so angry all of sudden? He had been so tender when she had first woken up, now he was back to being the sarcastic stranger of their first meeting.

Her chin rose to meet his challenge. 'I didn't specifically mean your mistress, I meant your family and friends in general. They must think it very strange the way you've suddenly taken yourself off to Norfolk.'

His hand still rested on the doorhandle, preparing to leave. 'My family and—friends know better than to question my movements.'

'Oh.'

'But I think I'll take up your suggestion and leave.'

'Oh, but——'

'Yes?' His eyes were narrowed.

Just that one word was enough to make the protest die in her throat. 'Nothing,' she mumbled, looking down at the nervous movements of her hands.

'A few days in London should be enough to deal

with any pressing—business that may have occurred in my absence.'

She felt really guilty now. 'Of course. I—I'm sorry if I've been a nuisance.'

He reached the bedside in two angry strides, grasping her arms painfully in his strong fingers. 'Stop feeling so damned sorry for yourself!' and he shook her.

'I'm sorry——'

'For God's sake stop it!' He pulled her sharply up against him, looking fiercely down at her, his breathing hard and erratic.

Time seemed to stand still as violet-blue eyes gazed up into deeply green ones, neither of them saying a word, Eve almost afraid to move. Close to like this she could see the gold flecks amongst the green of his eyes, could see how long and silky his lashes were, darkly so, a shadow across his jaw where he was in need of a shave. She could also smell the potent aroma of his aftershave, his basically male smell that attacked the senses, making her feel almost dizzy.

'Bart . . .' Was that aching sound really her voice? It sounded totally unlike her. Bart obviously thought so too, as he thrust her away from him.

'Get some sleep,' he ordered tersely. 'I'll be back from London in a few days. If you need me for anything Derek has my telephone number there.'

Then he was gone, the door closing firmly behind him. Eve stared at that door for several minutes, willing him to come back. But he didn't, and finally it was the tears that came, deep, racking sobs that had soaked her pillow within minutes.

How had it happened? Why had it happened? *When* had it happened? When had she fallen in love with Bart Jordan? Or had her antagonism towards him always been leading to this, had she sensed this danger from the first and run from it?

How, why, or even when it had happened was no longer important. It was a fact, she had fallen in love with another Carl, another man who had no interest in marrying 'a girl like her'. But at least Bart had been totally honest from the beginning, had made it clear he wanted to go to bed with her and nothing else. Then why had he suddenly changed? Just now she had been practically begging him to kiss her, and he had pushed her away from him.

Maybe he was no longer interested in her in that way, not now that her body ached for his. Since Carl she hadn't been physically attracted to any man, hadn't really been attracted in any way, her feelings seeming frozen. Now her heart had been laid bare to the love Bart had made her feel, a love he didn't want.

'What did you say to Bart to send him off to London in such a hurry?' Derek wanted to know the next day. 'You weren't being your usual bitchy self to him, were you?' he frowned. 'The poor man has hardly left your side since he brought you here.'

Eve had been listening to Nurse Evans chattering all morning about how Bart had sat with her most of the time, and quite frankly she was sick of hearing what a paragon he was. If he had really cared he would have stayed on. 'Why does everyone call him a "poor man"?' she asked waspishly. 'I'm the one that's been ill,' she added childishly.

'You're certainly back on form now,' Derek grinned. 'It's hard to believe after the way you've been this past week.'

'I feel fine,' she muttered. 'I just want to get out of here.'

Derek shook his head. 'Not yet, not for at least a week. Bart said that under no circumstances were you to leave here before he gets back.'

Everyone talked about Bart with such respect, she was surprised she hadn't noticed it before. But then maybe she had been blinded by prejudice. Maybe? She had! But the blinkers had been removed now, painfully so, and it wasn't helping the situation that everyone else seemed to have liked and respected him from the beginning. It just made her past behaviour seem more petty than she already knew it to be.

'Did he think I might?' she snapped.

'Yes,' came Derek's blunt reply.

Rebellion warred with the need to see Bart again, and finally that need won. 'Then he was wrong,' she said quietly, her eyes evasive as Derek gave her a sharp look. 'I've risked my health once,' she excused. 'I'm not about to do it again.'

'Good girl!' He squeezed her hand.

Her mouth twisted. She wasn't being 'good' at all. Right now she was being bad, very bad. She desperately wanted to see Bart, to be with him. Over the next few days that need deepened, so much so that she just longed for his return.

She was much better now, got out of bed in the mornings and dressed herself in the clothes that she had amazingly found filled most of the wardrobe, had washed her long hair, brushing it until it hung soft and silky over her shoulders. Her light make-up added colour to her cheeks, and she knew that despite how ill she had been for a time she was now ready to leave. And still Bart hadn't returned. He had been gone four days already, when would he come back? And when he did would it just be to say goodbye to her?

On the sixth day after Bart's departure the doctor gave her her discharge. And still Bart hadn't returned. She wasn't even going to see him again before she left!

'Why so glum?' Derek asked as he came to collect her. 'I thought you'd be glad to get out of this place.'

'I am,' she replied jerkily, forcefully packing her clothes away in her suitcase. 'Although everyone has been very kind,' she added grudgingly. 'About the bill——'

'Bart's taken care of it,' he dismissed.

Eve sighed, stopping to look up at him. 'Don't you think I owe him enough already?'

Derek shrugged. 'He wanted to pay for it.'

'That really isn't the point——'

'Talk to him about it, Eve,' he cut in firmly. 'I wouldn't presume to discuss it with him.'

She could see that Derek would be no match against the much more forceful Bart. 'You'd better give me his telephone number, then,' she said moodily. 'I'll call him.' She closed her suitcase with a firm snap.

Derek frowned. 'No need for that.'

'I have to,' she insisted, pushing her hair back over her shoulder, the black off-the-shoulder gypsy-style blouse and pencil-thin camel-coloured skirt showing off her slender curves, slightly thinner than she had been the last time she had worn the outfit. Her shoulders were left bare, tanned a golden brown from her afternoons of sunbathing on her boat earlier in the summer. She looked cool and beautiful, her sophisticated clothes giving her confidence. 'He's been more than generous already.' She took a last look around the room to make sure she hadn't forgotten anything, going through to the adjoining bathroom to check there too.

'That wasn't what I meant.' Derek stood in the doorway, moving back as she came into the main room. 'I meant you don't have to call Bart, you can tell him.'

She gave him an impatient glance. 'How?'

'Well, he's outside——'

'*Bart* is?' she stiffened.

'Mm,' Derek nodded. 'He's talking to the doctor.'

Eve dropped down weakly on to the bed. 'When did he get back?' she asked dazedly.

'Late last night.'

'Oh. I—I didn't think he was coming back.'

'Apparently he's been very busy. He looks it too. There must be more to being a wealthy banker than I realised,' Derek added with humour.

Eve wasn't really listening to him. Bart was back, was just outside talking to the doctor. She could hardly believe it. She had felt so miserable as she got ready to leave this morning, hadn't been the picture of health and happiness of a girl about to leave hospital.

Now she felt glowing, her eyes a deep sparkling blue in her anticipation of seeing Bart again after all this time.

Would he be cold towards her, as he had been before going to London? Oh, she hoped not.

'Derek——'

The door opened and Bart and the doctor came into the room. Eve ate him with her eyes, although he didn't even spare her a glance. He looked so handsome, the dark brown shirt and cream trousers casual in the extreme, and yet on Bart they looked immaculate. He was the sort of man who could wear denims and still walk into any company and be the most handsome and distinguished man there.

His hair was golden blond, but she could see several strands of grey among its thickness. She could also see deep lines of cynicism about his eyes and the firmness of his mouth. But he looked so good to her, so handsome, that she couldn't take her eyes off him.

'Ready to leave us?' Julian Reeve smiled at her.

She had come to like this young doctor over the last

few days, returning his smile warmly. She was in such a good mood now that Bart was here that she would probably have smiled at the devil himself if he were here. 'More than ready,' she nodded agreement eagerly.

He shook her hand firmly. 'And take better care of yourself.'

'She will.' Bart spoke for the first time, his tone curt.

'Fine,' the doctor nodded. 'I'll leave you now.'

'How are you?' Bart asked Eve once the doctor had left them.

'I'm well,' she replied stiltedly, her manner as stiff as his in her excitement at seeing him again.

'I'll take this out to the car,' Derek indicated the suitcase. 'See you outside.'

Eve didn't even notice his departure, still having eyes only for Bart. Derek was right, he did look tired. And she couldn't help wondering if his mistress had helped to make him that way. Jealousy ripped through her as she thought of the unknown woman.

Bart looked her over critically. 'You really are feeling better?' he probed.

'Yes,' her voice was husky.

'Good,' his tone was brisk. 'Then we'd better be going. You feel up to the drive?'

Eve frowned. 'It's only a few miles. I'm not made of glass, Bart.'

'Hampshire is more than a "few" miles.' His mouth twisted. 'It's going to take us several hours to get there. But you can sleep on the back seat if you're tired.'

'Hampshire?' she repeated dazedly. 'But——'

'Of course.' He sighed. 'Derek hasn't told you, has he?'

'Told me what?' she demanded, wondering what sort

of plans had been made behind her back.

'That you're coming home with me,' Bart told her calmly. 'To my house in Hampshire.'

She swallowed hard. 'I—I am?'

'Yes,' he nodded abruptly. 'You're going to have that rest I wanted you to have in the first place. You'll be staying with me for at least a month, maybe longer.'

CHAPTER SIX

'I—I WILL?' she stammered, overwhelmed by this sudden gift of time with him when she had thought she would never see him again.

Green eyes sharpened on her pale face. 'Are you sure you're feeling better?'

'Yes!' Her tone was indignantly impatient now.

'If you say so,' he shrugged, but still he frowned. 'No argument about the Hampshire idea?'

'No.'

'Why not?' he asked abruptly.

Eve shrugged. 'I need the rest.'

Bart raised his eyebrows. 'You're very meek all of a sudden,' he said thoughtfully.

Her eyes sparkled with anger. 'And you don't like me to be meek,' she recalled. 'I'll have to remember that.'

Some of the harshness left his face. 'When you want to annoy me, hmm?'

'Yes,' she snapped. If he preferred antagonism then that was exactly what he was going to get.

'That's better,' Bart grinned, taking hold of her elbow. 'Let's go, Derek's waiting for us.'

Derek was waiting beside the dark limousine Eve had been given a lift in the first night she had met Bart, although the chauffeur was noticeably absent. Derek sat in the back, the dividing window wound down, and Eve sat beside Bart in the front. He drove the huge car confidently.

He turned as he saw her questioning look. 'You're wondering why I don't drive myself all the time,' he mused.

Eve flushed at his ability to be able to read her mind. She would have to be careful of that, it wouldn't do for him to guess she was in love with him. 'Yes,' she confirmed tautly.

'I usually work in the back on the drive to and from work,' he explained.

'You work too hard,' she said without thinking, hearing Derek's snort of disbelief from the back and realising he thought she had been too outspoken. 'Sorry,' she mumbled. 'It's none of my business when you choose to work.'

'No, it isn't,' he agreed tersely.

They dropped Derek off at the hotel he and Judy had been staying at. 'I have my own car here,' he explained at Eve's dismayed look. 'We'll be driving back to London later today. Give me a call when you feel like having visitors,' he grinned at her, his eyes twinkling mischievously.

'Eve won't be in a prison.' Bart had obviously picked up Derek's mocking tone, scowling heavily. 'No one is making her accept these arrangements.' He turned to give her a dark look. 'Would you rather go to a nursing home?'

'No,' she shook her head firmly.

'Very well.' His hard gaze returned to Derek. 'Visit Eve any time you like,' he said in an offhand voice. 'She won't be going anywhere.'

Derek looked a little sheepish. 'I only meant——'

'It isn't important,' Bart cut in impatiently. 'I'd like to get going now, I have a dinner engagement this evening.'

Eve stiffened at his mention of a dinner engagement, managing to turn and wave to Derek out of the back window, her smile brittle and meaningless. Who was Bart having dinner with this evening? Was he just going to leave her in his house in Hampshire and go off to London to be with his mistress? She couldn't bear that, she would rather become his mistress herself than let that happen.

'Well?' he suddenly rasped.

She blinked at the suddenness of the question. 'Well what?'

'What's wrong?' he sighed. 'You haven't said a word for the past ten minutes.'

'I didn't know I was here to provide you with entertainment,' she said waspishly.

He grinned. 'This car may be big, but it isn't big enough for the form of entertainment I enjoy.'

Eve blushed scarlet. 'I suppose that's where you're going tonight,' she snapped. 'Tell me, purely for interest's sake, does she have a round bed or just a king-size one?'

'Purely for interest's sake,' Bart drawled, 'what the hell are you talking about?'

'You know,' she said moodily.

'I would hardly be asking if I did,' he scorned. 'And I wish I knew what bed sizes had to do with the business dinner I'm attending this evening.'

She blushed. 'Business dinner?'

'Yes,' he nodded. 'What did you think it was, an assignation with my mistress?'

'Well, you said you had one!'

He raised his eyebrows. 'Did I?'

'You know you did!' She was beginning to feel stupid now, a stupid jealous female. And if she weren't careful Bart would realise that was exactly what she was. 'The first night we met you said——'

'I believe I said a lot of things that night,' he recalled harshly. 'But then you were at your most provocative that night.'

'Does that mean you don't have a mistress?' She held her breath as she waited for his answer.

'I wouldn't say that,' he said noncommittally. 'What's the matter, Miss Icicle Heart, don't you like other people to enjoy themselves?' he taunted.

Her hands clenched together in her lap, and she only just stopped herself from hitting him. Loving this man didn't make him any less the arrogant tease he was.

'You can do what the hell you please,' she told him heatedly. 'And I don't have an icicle heart!'

'Then maybe you don't have a heart at all,' he dismissed scathingly.

'You were right the first time, the day you cancelled my concert. I've been hurt before,' she recalled dully, 'and I don't intend repeating the experience.' But she had, she had! And she had never admitted her past disillusionment to anyone.

'Tell me about him.' Bart's jaw was rigid, his gaze fixed firmly on the road in front of him.

'He—I—No,' she refused jerkily, 'I can't. I never talk about him.'

'Why?'

'Why? I—Well——'

'Does he still mean so much to you?' Bart rasped.

'No!' her denial was emphatic. 'No, it isn't that,' she said more calmly. 'He's just a painful, embarrassing experience that I would rather forget.'

'How old were you when he happened?' Bart asked dispassionately, as if he were clinically interested in the heartbreak she had suffered.

'Almost twenty,' she revealed tightly. 'Old enough to know better than to get involved with a man like him. I suppose we all have to find out the hard way.'

'And the affair was your way?'

'There was no affair!' she flared. 'At least, not in the way you mean.' She blushed as he turned, his piercing gaze probing her flushed features.

He shrugged. 'What other way is there? Either you did sleep with him or you didn't. Did you?' he rapped out.

'Yes. No! I—Mind your own business!' She turned away, staring sightlessly out of the window.

'Don't you know?' he taunted mockingly.

Pain flickered across her face before it was quickly hidden. 'Of course I know,' she answered in a controlled voice. 'I know all too well the way your current mistress feels——'

'We weren't discussing me,' he cut in abruptly.

'What's the matter?' she scorned. 'Don't you want to see it from the woman's point of view? To know the humiliation of being the person you go to when you have a spare hour or two and feel like spending them in bed? To——'

'That's enough!' he ordered tightly.

Eve gave a taunting laugh. 'You really don't want to hear it, do you?' she sneered. 'Well, you're going to!' She turned in her seat to face him, tense as a coiled spring. 'Whoever the woman in your life is she probably feels exactly as I did. You go to her, spend a few hours of forgetfulness in her arms before going back to your work and family, forgetting her until the next time you feel like going to bed with her. What you haven't considered—or perhaps you have and it just doesn't bother you—is that once you've gone she's going to realise she was just a body in a bed to you, and she'll hate you for it. Until the next time, when she'll love you again. Do you have any idea of how degrading that feeling can be?'

'No,' he ground out. 'But you obviously do.'

'Oh yes,' she acknowledged shrilly, 'I know. And no man will ever do that to me again!'

'This man—the man you were involved with—did he——' For once Bart seemed to have trouble articulating, his hands gripping the steering-wheel until his knuckles showed white.

'Yes, that's the way he treated me,' she snapped bitterly. 'And I was too damned stupid to realise until it was too late. You see, at nineteen, I still thought there was such a thing as love——' Her voice broke. 'I hadn't met anyone like you then.'

Bart turned to look at her briefly, his skin pulled taut across his hard cheekbones. 'What the hell do I have to do with the way this man treated you?'

Her mouth twisted. 'Have you forgotten the relationship you offered me the first night we met?'

A ruddy hue coloured his cheeks. 'You made me angry—'

Her harsh laugh cut into his explanation. '*I* made you angry?' she scorned. 'What do you think you did to me? You insulted me in the worst way possible, thought I should just be grateful you had noticed me.'

'Eve——'

'Don't deny it, Bart.' She shook her head, biting her bottom lip.

'Okay,' he snapped, 'I won't deny that I insulted you, but the second part is completely untrue. And I'm nothing like the man you got yourself involved with——'

'I didn't involve myself with him,' she gasped. 'I fell in love with him.'

'And by the sound of it he already had a wife and family!'

'Something he kept very quiet about, I can tell you,' she said fiercely. 'But then, men like you are all the same——'

'Will you stop likening me to the swine who hurt you!'

'But you are like him,' she said dully. She had forgotten for a while, had wanted to forget because she had fallen in love with him. But in the end he was going to hurt her as much as Carl had—more so, because she loved Bart as a woman, and not with the calf-love she had felt towards Carl.

Strange, she could see it that way now. At the time it had had the effect of changing her whole life, and now it meant nothing to her, less than nothing. Oh, she regretted that part of her life, hated the fact that Carl had made love to her, but the past couldn't be changed, it could only be accepted. And she thought she was finally doing that.

But men like Bart still didn't marry 'girls like her', and any relationship she had with him would be as transient as it had been with Carl. Could she accept *that*? When she had the answer to that she would be able to start living again.

She noticed Bart struggling beside her to light a cheroot. 'Let me,' she offered instantly.

He leant forward as she struck the lighter, instantly surrounded by a thick cloud of smoke. 'Thanks,' he said tersely, pocketing the lighter. 'I'm sorry if you think I'm like this other man,' he added abruptly.

'Bart——'

'Let's just forget it, Eve,' he told her coldly. 'You're going to be my guest for the next few weeks, so let's just try and be polite to each other. I should be away a lot of the time, anyway.'

Her eyes widened. 'You actually live at this house in Hampshire?'

'You thought I lived in London?'

'Well, I—Yes.'

'Sorry to disappoint you,' his mouth twisted, 'but I shall be home to dinner every evening, with the exception of tonight, and I shall be there every weekend too.' He quirked an eyebrow at her. 'Changed your mind?'

'No,' she answered instantly.

'Brave of you,' he taunted.

'Not really,' she returned coolly. 'I'm sure you like your women to be in good health. And that you don't like them to be skinny.'

Bart threw back his head and laughed, his teeth very white and even. 'That rankled, hmm?'

'A little,' she nodded. 'I've lost a little weight lately——'

'More than a little, Eve,' he put in softly.

'Yes,' she sighed. 'You'll just have to fatten me up— My chocolates!' she cried in dismay. 'They're still on the boat. My flowers too.'

'They'll still be there when you get back.'

'But my flowers will be dead!'

'I'll get you some more,' he said easily. 'Deep pink carnations, right?'

Her eyes widened. 'How did you know that?'

Bart shrugged. 'I asked Derek.'

There had been a vase of deep pink carnations in her hospital room every day, and she realised now that Bart must have arranged that. There had been no card on them, and Derek denied all knowledge, and so she had assumed the service came in with the room. She felt a warm glow deep inside her that it had been Bart sending them to her.

'Did you get all your work in London done?' she asked now.

'Most of it. Don't tell me it bothered you that I was gone so long?' he taunted.

Eve flushed, not about to admit to it now. 'Not particularly. Although I was a little worried who was going to pay the bill,' she added mischievously.

He gave a deep chuckle. 'All taken care of.'

'Bart——'

'Not now, Eve,' he dismissed, obviously guessing

what she was going to say. 'It's part of a business manager's job to take care of such things.'

'But——'

'Some other time, Eve,' he said wearily. 'I've had enough of business the last few days, and I have that dinner this evening.'

'If you're tired I could always drive for a while,' she offered tentatively.

His mouth quirked with humour. 'You think you could handle a car like this?'

She grimaced. 'I could try.'

'No,' he shook his head. 'It's time you took a rest.' He drew the car on to the side of the road. 'In the back,' he instructed.

'I——'

'Do it, Eve,' he said firmly. 'The doctor said you are to rest as much as possible for the next week or so. Arguing with me isn't restful,' he added dryly.

For a moment she looked rebellious, but the implacability of his expression was enough to tell her that if she didn't get into the back Bart was likely to carry her there.

She gave an angry sigh, her mouth set in an angry line as she saw Bart's smile of satisfaction as she got into the back of the car. He had too much of his own way, which probably accounted for his arrogance. Well, she wasn't going to be a complacent guest!

He manoeuvred the car back into the flow of traffic, the engine just a purr in the background. 'Lie down and get some sleep,' he ordered.

'I'm not in the least sleepy,' she snapped.

He grinned at her in the driving mirror, instantly looking younger. 'You will be if you lie down.'

She did so reluctantly. 'Do you order your employees about in this way?' she asked moodily.

'I don't usually need to,' he drawled.

'No,' she scorned softly, determined he wasn't going to have things all his own way, 'I suppose you just crack the whip and everyone runs to your bidding.'

Bart scowled. 'You have a sharp tongue, Eve. Careful someone doesn't try to blunt the edges.'

'You?' she taunted, enjoying baiting him.

'No, not me,' he said harshly. 'Now get some sleep.' He closed the window between them.

She hadn't thought she could possibly sleep with Bart so close to her but somehow the movement of the car and the soft hum of the engine caused her to drift into a dreamless sleep. She opened her eyes with a start, sitting up to find they had stopped at a roadside café, and Bart was sitting patiently in the front of the car waiting for her to wake up.

She sat up, blinking foggily. 'Have I been asleep long?' she murmured sleepily.

'About an hour.' Bart turned to smile at her, the window now wound down between them. His smile widened as he looked at her. 'You look like a scarecrow,' he chuckled. 'Here,' he handed her the comb from his back pocket, still grinning.

Eve scowled at him, ignoring the comb. 'I have a brush in my bag.' She searched through its contents for the brush, disgruntled at being told she looked like a scarecrow. How did he expect her to look, as if she had stepped out of a fashion magazine?

'Amongst other things,' he taunted as she had trouble finding her brush. He looked very relaxed and handsome as he watched her, not at all like a man who had been driving in heavy traffic for the last two hours.

She held up her brush triumphantly, brushing her long hair with smooth strokes. 'There's nothing in that bag that isn't a necessity,' she told him haughtily.

His eyebrows rose mockingly. 'Then you must have

a lot of necessities.' He eyed the handbag. 'That looks more like a suitcase!'

She put the brush away, closing the maligned handbag with a firm snap. 'Less like a scarecrow?' she looked at him steadily.

'You take offence too easily.' He swung out of the car, opening the door for her. 'You always look beautiful, and you know it,' he told her as she stepped out beside him.

She looked up at him teasingly, her bad humour fading as the last of the sleepy fog left her. 'Even soaking wet and covered in mud?'

There was no answering smile from him. 'No,' he said heavily, 'you didn't look beautiful then. You looked—God, you looked dead!' He had gone very pale under his tan.

'But I'm not,' she pointed out gently, realising what a shock it must have been when he had thought he had found her, anyone, dead. 'I am hungry, though,' she added to break the tension she had unwittingly reintroduced.

'Now I know you're feeling better,' he smiled, taking her hand into the warmth of his. 'Let's go and feed you.'

Her fingers curled pleasurably about his, knowing he was only holding her to help her across the uneven surface of the car park to the café. Once inside his arm went about her waist, guiding her to a table in the corner of the noisy café.

'I hate these places,' he grimaced, leaning over the table as Eve moved along the bench seat to make room for him.

Eve grinned. 'Snob!' she teased him.

'Not at all,' he answered seriously. 'I just hate the way they massacre food so that it's unrecognisable as what you ordered. I'm not sure what I'll bring you back to eat, and the tea and coffee both taste the same, so it doesn't really matter which one of them I choose.'

Eve spluttered with laughter at his expression of disgust. 'You are a snob.'

'Maybe—about food. Just think what that combination of tea and coffee will do to my body.'

Thinking about his body in any way made her blush. 'I'll have the tea,' she said stiltedly. 'And anything else you feel brave enough to try.'

He gave a grunt of acknowledgment, walking over to the self-service area. Eve could watch him unguarded now, could drink in the sight of him, the way he stood head and shoulders above any other man in the room, his blond good looks and haughty bearing adding to his air of distinction. He looked totally out of place in this noisy, untidy roadside café, the young girl behind the serving counter obviously thinking so too, spending more time with him than was necessary, much to the annoyance of the other people waiting to be served.

He chatted in a friendly manner to the girl taking the money, and Eve found herself disliking the way the pretty redhead flirted with him. He would attract female attention wherever he went, probably even in thirty years' time, and Eve resented that attention.

She was frowning when he returned to their table with the laden tray, putting a plate of roast chicken, creamed potatoes and peas in front of her. Eve ate it automatically, barely noticing the half-cold food. Would it always be like this, would she always feel this burning jealousy of any other woman in the same room as Bart? If she did she was in for a miserable time of it.

'It isn't that good,' Bart broke into her thoughts. 'In fact it isn't good at all.' He thrust his own plate away half eaten. 'It's worse that usual. You must be hungrier than we realised,' he grimaced.

Eve looked up at him, blinking dazedly, her thoughts having been far away. 'I must?'

He looked pointedly at her almost empty plate. 'If you were able to eat that you must have been hungry.'

She looked down at the plate too. All she had left were the peas, something she didn't like anyway. And she hadn't tasted a thing, hadn't been aware of eating anything!

She pushed the plate away, drinking down the cold tea/coffee. 'I'm ready to leave now if you are.'

'I was ready to leave before I came in, I just thought you should eat something. Do you want a dessert?'

'No, no, thank you.'

Bart frowned at her stilted manner. 'Have I upset you by criticising the food?' he probed.

'No, of course not.' She gave a bright smile. 'You were right, it is awful.'

'Then let's go.' He stood, helping her to her feet.

Eve removed her arm from his grasp as quickly as she could without appearing rude, but even so his eyes narrowed questioningly. 'Aren't you hungry?' she asked nervously. 'You haven't eaten a thing.'

'It won't do me any harm. I've had too many business lunches lately. I wouldn't want to get a middle-aged paunch,' he added lightly.

There wasn't much likelihood of that; his stomach taut and flat, his physical fitness was in no doubt.

She had a feeling this convalescence at Bart's home was going to be a form of torture for her, wanting him and not able to have him. His manner had been friendly today, but nothing like it had been in the past. And she knew what was missing, Bart was no longer attracted to her. He was courteous, even kind, but there was no desire in his behaviour. She had killed all that with her coldness.

They were soon back on the road going towards

Hampshire, Bart refusing her offer to drive. She would have been nervous driving this monster of a car anyway, but she had felt she ought to make the offer. She hoped she hadn't looked too relieved when Bart refused, although by the amusement in his eyes she thought she probably had.

'My concerts,' she broached tentatively. 'Why did you arrive and leave at strange times?'

He quirked an eyebrow. 'Did it upset you?'

She flushed. 'Not upset—annoyed, perhaps. I don't appreciate my audience leaving before the end of a performance, or walking in halfway through the show.'

Bart turned to grin at her. 'Much as I would like it to be the case, *you* aren't my only business interest. I had meetings and dinners to attend.'

'I see.' So she was just a business interest! Bart couldn't have told her any more clearly that she came under the heading of business in his life. This convalescence at his home was just to get her back to work—for him. She had been naïve to think it was anything else.

The rest of the drive passed in silence. Bart's house was set in its own grounds, surrounded by trees and shrubs, the lawn kept smoothly green; a tennis-court was visible at the back of the house, as was a swimming-pool.

Eve had a chance to admire the house as they drove down the long gravel driveway, liking the way it had been designed with a much smaller country cottage in mind, wild roses climbing all over the front of the house.

'It's beautiful, Bart!' Her face glowed as she turned to him.

'I hoped you would like it. I find it a lot more

peaceful than living in town. People are less inclined to just call in here.'

Eve smiled. 'I can imagine they would be.' It was exactly the reason she lived in Norfolk.

He smiled back, taking her suitcase out of the boot. 'Come on, I'll introduce you to the most important woman in my life.'

Her smile faded. 'She lives *here*?'

'Yes,' Bart nodded, taking her arm in a firm grip and taking her into the house. 'Maisie!' he called, throwing his car keys on the hall table. 'Maisie, we're home!'

Eve barely noticed the comfort of Bart's home, the open-plan design, the easy-chairs and scatter rugs, the complete homeliness of their surroundings.

Bart had his mistress living here! Not an apartment in town at all, but here, in his own home, in the home he had invited her to share too!

'She's probably upstairs,' he told Eve. 'I'll just go up and get her.'

She felt more ill than ever now. Bart's mistress was probably upstairs all right, and she was probably waiting for him to join her. Oh, this was going to be awful!

She could hear the murmur of voices now, Bart's deep attractive tone and a light female one. God, she couldn't do this, this situation was going to be impossible. She had to get away from here—if only her feet weren't glued to this highly polished floor!

A woman appeared at the top of the stairs, a woman of at least fifty. No mistress this, although Bart's arm about her shoulders was evidence of his affection for her.

The woman walked down the stairs, a slight limp to her left leg, her iron-grey hair pulled back into a bun at her nape, her face weathered and lined, her body portly rather than plump. Bart followed behind her, the mockery in his dark green eyes openly taunting

Eve. He knew exactly what she had been thinking, had deliberately nurtured that impression.

'Hello, dear,' the woman called Maisie greeted her warmly. 'I'm sorry I wasn't down here when you arrived,' she limped over to where Eve still stood. 'I was just putting the finishing touches to your room.'

Eve swallowed hard. 'I—Thank you.'

'This is my housekeeper, Eve,' Bart drawled, obviously enjoying her confusion. 'Maisie is Adam's mother. You remember Adam?'

She remembered the chauffeur very well. 'Er—yes.' She put out her hand politely. 'I'm pleased to meet you, Mrs——'

'Maisie will do, dear,' the other woman said cheerfully. 'I've got no time for formality. Bart will tell you that,' she smiled at him fondly.

'Considering you almost brought me up I'd feel insulted if you called me Mr Jordan,' he said deeply. 'Now can we have one of your delicious teas, Maisie?' he requested eagerly, obviously feeling his lack of lunch now.

'Give me two minutes,' she nodded. 'And take Miss Meredith's case upstairs. She'd probably like to freshen up too.'

'Yes, Maisie.' He grinned at Eve. 'Come on, no one argues with Maisie's instructions.'

'Go on with you!' the housekeeper tutted. 'You've always been too bossy for your own good.'

Instead of the rival she had been expecting Eve now sensed an ally. 'You've noticed that too, have you, Maisie?' She eyed Bart challengingly.

Maisie snorted with laughter. 'Met your match, have you?' she taunted him. 'About time too.' She disappeared into what Eve presumed to be the kitchen.

Bart smiled with open amusement now. 'Not what you were expecting, is she?'

Eve refused to rise to his bait. 'Shouldn't you be taking me upstairs?'

'Okay.' He picked up her suitcase, still laughing at her. 'But maybe if you were a little less suspicious you wouldn't keep jumping to the wrong conclusions.'

'I'm not wrong about you.' She followed him up the stairs.

'Aren't you?' He was suddenly serious again.

She shook her head firmly. 'I don't think so.'

He shrugged. 'If you say so. Maisie has put you in the room opposite mine.' He pushed open the door, the one across the corridor firmly closed.

Eve blushed. 'I—She doesn't think——'

Bart's expression darkened as he moved into the bedroom to throw the suitcase down on top of the bed, his movements savage. He turned to face her, his eyes narrowed to steely slits, his stance challenging. 'Let's get one thing straight from the first, Eve,' he rasped in a controlled voice. 'You are here as my guest, nothing else. I have no intention of making that short trip across the corridor from my room to yours every night.'

'But Maisie . . .' she bit her lip.

'Maisie is well aware who you are and why you're here. This is my home, Eve,' he added harshly. 'I don't bring women here, not ones I intend sleeping with anyway. Maisie would have no hesitation in making her opinion of such an arrangement known. And I wouldn't insult her with such behaviour.'

He was furiously angry, she could see that. Bart didn't have the sort of temper that made him rant and rave at his opponent, he just became chillingly polite, his words rapier-sharp, his manner cold. She would have preferred a heated explosion of words, at least then she would have been able to retaliate. At the moment she just felt guilty for her suspicions.

She looked down at her feet. 'I'm sorry, I just didn't want you to think that I——'

'Don't add insult to injury,' he cut in curtly, his mouth twisted with distaste. 'I think you made your opinion of "men like me" very clear on the journey down here. After what you told me I wouldn't touch you even if I wanted to.'

'Which you don't.'

'Which I don't,' he confirmed harshly. 'You have enough bitterness inside you already without my adding to it.'

Eve flushed, her eyes sparkling angrily. 'I'm not bitter——'

'Yes, you are, damn you!' he snapped. 'How many men have you been out with the last five years?'

She glared at him rebelliously. 'A few.'

Bart's expression was at once scornful. 'And how many of them have been allowed to so much as kiss you?'

'I don't see that it's any of your business——'

'How many, Eve?' he repeated tautly.

'I—It—Only one,' she revealed tightly.

He gave a mocking laugh. 'I'm sure he considered himself highly privileged,' he said insultingly.

Her hands were clenched into fists at her sides, her blue eyes dark with pain. 'I don't know. Did you?' She faced him defiantly.

He frowned, searching her rebellious features with deep intensity. 'You're saying I was the first man to kiss you in five years?' he said slowly, disbelievingly.

'Yes!' she snapped.

'My God!' he breathed deeply.

Eve turned away, hating the pity in his eyes. 'I—I don't think I'll have any tea, thank you. I think I would rather stay up here and rest.'

'Have I upset you again?' he asked softly, gently.

'No.' She still stood with her back towards him. 'I—I'm just tired.' Which was true, but she was emotionally, not physically, tired.

Bart's hands came down gently on her shoulders. 'I'm sorry, Eve. I had no idea.'

She had to stop herself leaning back against the hardness of his body. 'Maisie will be expecting you for your tea,' she said jerkily, knowing that if he didn't soon leave she was going to burst into tears. 'Apologise for me.'

'I will.' His hands fell away, although she could still feel the imprint of his fingers on her naked shoulders. 'Get some sleep,' he advised abruptly. 'Everything will look different once you're rested.'

She just managed to wait until the door closed softly on his exit before the tears started to fall. Maybe some things would look different when she woke up, but one thing would never change. She was in love with Bart Jordan, and he no longer wanted her.

CHAPTER SEVEN

THE room was in darkness when she woke up, and her watch told her it was after eight, which meant she had been asleep over three hours. Bart would already have left for his dinner engagement, so at least she wouldn't have to face him when she got downstairs. His sharp gaze wouldn't have missed the slight puffiness around her eyes. She had cried herself to sleep, her face buried in the pillow so that no one should hear her sobs.

Bart knew more about her than Derek had managed to find out in the whole of the five years she had known him. She seemed to tell Bart things without actually meaning to, seemed to want him to know all about her disastrous past. At least this way he could never accuse her of holding anything back from him.

The door opened quietly and Maisie peeped inside the room. 'Ah, you're awake.' She came fully into the room, a wide smile lighting up her features. 'I just thought I'd look in on you, make sure you're all right.'

'I'm fine.' Eve turned from taking a pair of denims and cotton shirt-top out of the wardrobe she had unpacked them into earlier, unembarrassed in the bra and briefs she had slept in. After all, they were both women. Now if it had been Bart . . .!

'Bart's already gone out.' Maisie seemed to read her thoughts. 'He looked in on you before he went, but he said you were still fast asleep then.'

Colour flooded her cheeks. So Bart had seen her in the bra and briefs after all!

'I suppose you're feeling a little hungry now,' Maisie continued to talk as Eve dressed.

'Ravenous,' she admitted with a smile, aware that she was overstating somewhat.

'I've got some homemade soup downstairs, a nice tender steak and green salad. Bart said I was to keep it light but nutritious. There's strawberry shortcake for dessert.'

'It sounds lovely. I hope I'm not putting you to too much trouble having to cook for me like this.' Eve finished buttoning her shirt. 'I could always get my own dinner,' she offered tentatively.

'I wouldn't hear of it!' Maisie looked affronted. 'Besides, I usually cook for Bart. He very rarely has these business meetings in the evenings. It's just unfortunate that tonight should be one of those occasions.'

Eve frowned, tucking her shirt into her denims. 'But surely he—Bart often stays in town overnight?' She tidied the bed, now ready to go down and have that delicious-sounding dinner.

'Not that I recall,' Maisie shook her head. 'And I should know, I've looked after him here for the last four years, since his parents died.'

'I didn't know his parents were dead.' So Bart didn't stay in town, and he didn't bring his women here either. So when did he meet them?

'It was a boating accident.' The two women walked down the wide staircase together. 'On their second honeymoon, ironically enough.'

'How tragic!' And she meant it. What an awful thing to happen when it was supposed to be such a happy occasion. 'My own parents are dead too,' she revealed huskily.

'Then you and Bart have a common bond. Of course Bart has a sister, but she lives in America now.'

'I didn't realise.' She was learning more about Bart in these few brief minutes than she had in the rest of the time she had known him.

'She's lived there for about five years now. Bart misses the children, I know. They used to spend a lot of time here. Many's the time I've caught one of them sliding down the banisters,' Maisie recalled with a chuckle. 'Darren, he's the oldest boy, he's a lot like Bart was as a boy. It's like going back twenty-five years to see Darren here. Bart used to slide down the banisters too, amongst other things. He was a holy terror!'

It was strange to hear Bart talked of as a boy. He was such a self-assured, self-sufficient man that it was hard to believe he had ever suffered the awkwardness of being a teenager, the uncertainties of a first date, the first painful love affair.

The smile instantly left her face as she remembered how Carl had been her first and only love affair. And now she was in love with a man who could hurt her a hundred times more than Carl ever had.

'Bart usually eats in the small family dining-room,' Maisie told her. 'You go in and make yourself comfortable and I'll bring your soup through to you.'

'I—Could I possibly eat in the kitchen?' Eve looked pleadingly at the older woman. 'I don't feel like being alone at the moment.' When she was alone she thought too much, and usually about Bart.

'You come along into the kitchen with me, dear,' the housekeeper said warmly. 'Although Adam may come in later,' she warned.

Eve remembered the tall, dark-haired chauffeur, a man of about thirty, rather good-looking. 'You said he's your son,' she said interestedly, following Maisie into the huge spotlessly clean kitchen.

'Actually Bart told you that.' Maisie set about warming the soup. 'No, you sit down, Eve,' she was told as she went to lay the table. 'This won't take me a minute. Yes, Adam's my son.' She took a freshly baked loaf out of the cupboard. 'When my husband died it seemed only natural that Adam should take over from him as chauffeur. He and Bart grew up together. They're more like brothers than employer and employee.'

So the formality she had witnessed that first evening had been for her benefit. In private Adam probably called Bart by his first name like his mother did. Bart was proving to be a constant surprise to her.

'Do you and Adam live in the house?' Eve asked as she ate the delicious soup. It was years since she had had anything but the tinned variety, and this soup was a meal in itself. If all of Maisie's cooking was like this she wouldn't have any trouble putting on the pounds she had lost.

'I do, Adam doesn't.' Maisie was watching over the steak as it grilled. 'I have a flat at the back of the house, Adam has one over the garage.' She smiled. 'There are times when a man doesn't want his mother about.'

Eve laughed too. 'I suppose there are.'

'Bart said your aunt and uncle are in Egypt,' Maisie went on conversationally. 'It must be interesting work.'

Eve nodded. 'They like it.'

'Bart had terrible trouble trying to reach your uncle. I think he must have been disconnected half a dozen times.'

Her empty soup bowl was replaced by the steak and green salad. 'He's spoken to my uncle?' she asked dazedly.

Maisie frowned. 'Didn't you know? Bart must have forgotten to tell you. He's been so worried about you, and he's been working day and night so that he could get this nasty embezzling business cleared up before you came out of hospital.'

Eve was completely puzzled now. 'Embezzling?'

'Oh yes, dear.' Maisie sat down opposite her. 'One of Bart's employees had been taking money for the past year. And he was so clever at it that no one even realised he was doing it.'

So this was the reason Bart had been gone six days instead of the two or three he had first implied. 'I didn't know,' she said softly, wondering what else she didn't know.

'Bart wouldn't want to worry you when you've been so ill. But now that you are here perhaps he'll be able to take a few days off to be with you. He really does work too hard.'

'I doubt if my being here will stop him,' Eve said ruefully.

'I'm sure if you asked him he would.' Maisie gave her a coy look.

Eve bit her lip. 'I don't think you understand. Bart and I—We aren't——'

'What you are or aren't is none of my business,' the other woman said briskly. 'All I know is that you're the first woman he's seen fit to bring home in all the time I've known him, and that's over thirty years.'

'Oh, but I—I work for Bart,' Eve desperately tried to explain her role in Bart's life, for all she wished it could be different. 'The doctor said I should continue to rest, so Bart brought me here to make sure I do.'

'He could have done that in one of those fancy clinics,' Maisie dismissed.

'Oh, but——'

'Eat your dinner, Eve,' she was told firmly.

Bart was right, no one argued with Maisie's instructions!

Her thoughts were all of Bart as she ate. He must be very discreet if even the astute Maisie didn't know about the women in his life. Although the housekeeper hadn't exactly said there hadn't been any, just that she had never met them. Bart was obviously very fond of Maisie, so perhaps he was just being thoughtful by not introducing her to any of his women friends.

Adam came into the kitchen as she was halfway through the huge piece of strawberry shortcake his mother had given her. He hesitated in the doorway as he saw her sitting at the kitchen table looking quite at home, his mother sitting opposite her drinking coffee.

'Well, don't just stand there,' his mother encouraged. 'You're letting moths into the room.'

Still he hesitated, obviously unsure of Eve's reaction to him coming inside.

'Join us for coffee, won't you?' she invited with a smile. 'And you really should have some of this shortcake, it's delicious,' she added enticingly.

A smile lit his handsome features as he came in and closed the door. Out of his uniform he wore a casual checked shirt and faded denims, and he looked younger than his thirty-two years.

Maisie stood up, smiling fondly at her son. 'I suppose now Eve's suggested it you would like something to eat?'

'Just the shortcake will be fine.' He put his hands in his back pockets. 'I ate earlier.'

'I can imagine,' his mother derided. 'Well, stop cluttering up my kitchen and sit down. Eve doesn't bite, do you, dear?'

Eve had to hold back a smile at Adam's obvious embarrassment. Maisie really was incorrigible—but very likeable. She loved her already. 'I haven't been known to,' she smiled sympathetically at Adam. 'But there's always a first time. Please sit down, Adam.'

He did so, although he still looked uncomfortable. 'I saw one of your concerts in London, Miss Meredith,' he finally spoke.

'Please call me Eve,' she invited.

He flushed with pleasure. 'I really enjoyed your show, Eve.'

'Thank you,' she accepted.

'Bart tells me you won't be doing any more, so I'm glad I got to see you.'

She frowned. 'Bart told you that?'

'Well, of course he did,' Maisie scorned. 'Anyone can see just by looking at you that you aren't suited to that sort of life.'

Bart had told these people, obviously his friends, that her career was at an end—then why hadn't he told her? There seemed to be quite a few things he hadn't enlightened her about, including the telephone call to her uncle. She wondered what Uncle George had made of receiving a telephone call from a complete stranger. No doubt Bart had made it all seem perfectly natural, he seemed to have that effect on most people.

She enjoyed her evening with the Merricks, joining in a goodnatured game of cards with Adam. He had thawed towards her as the evening progressed, and the two of them were now firm friends.

'It's lucky for you we aren't playing strip-poker.' He sat back in his chair, grinning as he won yet another game. 'You'd be stark naked by now.'

'Adam!' his mother reproved. 'Eve's still Bart's guest, even if she doesn't mind spending time with you.'

'Very true, Maisie.' Bart stood in the doorway out to the hall, pulling impatiently at the bow-tie at his throat. Cold green eyes were turned on Eve. 'I didn't expect to find you in here. It's after eleven, you should be in bed,' he said abruptly.

She had missed him this evening, had been looking forward to seeing him, but she instantly saw red at his arrogant tone. 'I'll go to bed when I'm ready,' she snapped, ignoring how handsome he looked in the dark evening clothes, his blond hair slightly ruffled by the light breeze outside.

'It's my fault, Bart,' Adam packed away the cards. 'I was so enjoying winning that I forgot Eve hasn't been well.'

'I'm perfectly all right,' she defended. 'And I'm quite capable of deciding when I should go to bed.' She gave Bart a defiant look.

He ignored her, talking to Maisie. 'Could I have a tray of coffee in my study?'

'You aren't working this time of night?' she instantly scolded.

'Yes,' he confirmed curtly. 'And make the coffee strong, Maisie. I think I'm going to need it.' He turned on his heel and walked away, and a door slammed with controlled force several seconds later.

Eve looked down at her hands, blinking back the tears. She was responsible for Bart's bad mood. If only he hadn't spoken to her like that!

Adam stood up noisily. 'Time I went, I think.'

Eve looked up guiltily. 'It's all my fault,' she choked. 'I didn't mean to anger him, but——'

'You didn't, child,' Maisie soothed. 'He's just over-worked and tired. I'll make the coffee, and then you can take it in to him and the two of you can make your peace.'

Eve flushed as she realised how Maisie expected them to 'make their peace'. The older woman obviously expected them to be in each other's arms as soon as the study door was closed. If only that were the truth! But the real truth was that they would probably end up arguing, as they usually did.

But she didn't like to disappoint the other woman, so she obediently took the tray of coffee to Bart's study.

'Come!' came the barked command at her tentative

knock. He didn't seem surprised to see her. 'Maisie never knocks,' he explained dryly, making room on the cluttered desk for her to put the tray down.

She did so, running her hands nervously down her thighs. 'I'm sorry about earlier,' she said awkwardly. 'You won't be angry with Adam, will you?'

'You like him?' he answered her question with one of his own, pouring coffee into the two cups Maisie had put on the tray and drinking his black.

Eve frowned. 'I—Yes, I like him.'

'Maybe you would have preferred it if you had been playing strip-poker,' he said coldly.

She gasped. 'You heard that?'

Bart's mouth twisted, his black evening jacket now discarded, his shirt partly unbuttoned, the cuffs turned back to just below the elbows. 'Yes, I heard,' he drawled. 'When I brought you here I didn't expect you to get involved with Adam.'

'I'm not involved——'

'He's attracted to you, and you say you like him.' He shrugged dismissively, leaning back in the comfortable chair that stood behind the huge mahogany desk. Books covered every wall, a sofa the same leather as the chair was placed in front of the unlit fireplace.

'I like him, yes,' Eve said impatiently. 'But not like—not like——' she bit her lip, realising how close she had come to telling him of her love for him.

'Not like the man from your past,' he finished in a chilling voice. 'Don't you think five years is enough time to have got over him?'

'I am over him!' she insisted vehemently.

'But don't mean to ever forget what he did to you,' Bart scorned, standing up to flex his tired back muscles.

He did look very tired, she could see that now. 'Do you have to do that work this evening?' she asked concernedly. 'It's very late, and——'

'And I do have to do it,' he abruptly sat down again. 'My assistant turned out to be a crook, and now I have to double check everything he's ever been involved in.'

Her eyes widened. 'Your assistant was the embezzler?'

His mouth twisted. 'Maisie told you.'

Eve flushed. 'She—she seems to think we're good friends. I tried to explain, but——'

'Maisie is a romantic at heart,' he mocked.

'She's a very genuine person,' Eve defended indignantly. 'I like her very much.'

He nodded. 'Most people do. Sit down and drink your coffee,' he invited tersely.

She did so, watching as he bent over the papers on his desk. 'Couldn't someone else do that?' she ventured after several minutes' silence.

Bart looked up, blinking to focus on her. He put his gold pen down, leaning back with a sigh. 'After the way Sean let me down I'm not sure I can trust someone else to do it. He'd been with me ten years. I never would have believed it of him if I hadn't been the one to discover his discrepancies.'

'I'm sorry.' It sounded as if Sean had been a personal friend as well as an employee.

'So am I,' he said heavily, running a hand around the back of his neck.

'Does it ache?'

'Mm?' he frowned his puzzlement.

'Your nape, does it ache?'

'Yes,' Bart sighed.

'Would you like me to——' she broke off. 'No, never mind.' She looked away, blushing.

'Would I like you to . . .?' he prompted softly.

She looked down at her hands, wishing she had never started this. 'My uncle—he often gets an ache there, it comes from bending down so much, I think.

Anyway,' she licked her dry lips, 'I usually—massage it for him.'

'You do?'

Eve swallowed hard. 'Yes.'

He sat back. 'Feel free,' he invited.

Her lashes fluttered up, confusion in her violet-blue eyes. 'You—you want me to massage your neck for you?'

'If you wouldn't mind,' he nodded.

She didn't mind, but the thought of touching him unnerved her somewhat. What if she should betray her feelings towards him?

'If you would rather not,' he sensed her hesitation, once again picking up his pen. 'I should get on with this anyway.'

'No! I mean—I'll massage your neck for you.' She stood up, moving to the back of his chair. The warm vibrancy of him reached out to her, and she knew she had let herself in for a subtle form of torture.

'Are you all right back there?' Bart queried as she made no move to touch him.

'If you could just lean back . . .'

He did so, and Eve's fingers fluttered down on to his broad shoulders, feeling the tension in his muscles. He felt good to touch, firm and smooth, and her fingers began to love their set task.

'You're good,' Bart murmured pleasurably.

'I—Thank you.'

She swallowed hard as he leant his head back against her breasts, his hair very blond against the black shirt she wore. Her fingers ached to caress the silky hair visible in the deep vee of his shirt, her nails digging into the flesh of his shoulders as she resisted the impulse.

'Hey,' Bart chided softly, his eyes closed, 'that hurts!'

'Sorry.' Her hands were instantly removed, but she couldn't move away, Bart's head was heavy against her breasts. He was moving sensuously against her now, and Eve was almost afraid to breathe in case he stopped the movement.

'I could quite easily go to sleep against you,' he murmured.

'It wouldn't be very comfortable for me,' she said breathlessly.

He glanced up at her flushed features. 'No, I suppose not.' He sat forward, standing up to take her hand and lead her over to the sofa, gently pushing her down in one corner, sitting down beside her to rest his head in exactly the same position as before. 'Mm,' he sat up again after a few minutes. 'Not comfortable enough.'

'What are you doing?' she demanded as he slipped her shoes off and put her feet up on the sofa.

'Move over,' he instructed, switching off the main light, just leaving the desk-lamp on.

Eve gazed up at him with apprehensive eyes. 'Move over . . .?'

'Yes.' He lay down beside her, his lean length moulded to her slender curves on the narrow width of the sofa, his arm about her waist. 'Comfortable?' he snuggled into the warm softness of her breasts.

Strangely enough, she was. But she couldn't stay here, it was too dangerous. But oh, how nice it was to lie here with Bart, not to be arguing with him but for once to be in complete harmony.

'I would have suggested we go up to bed,' he said sleepily, 'but I didn't think you would agree to that.'

She wasn't so sure about that. Right now she was feeling very vulnerable towards him, and this closeness was reducing her resistance to nil. But Bart didn't seem to have seduction in mind, for his arm about her waist soon relaxed, his even breathing telling her he was asleep.

Eve was at last able to relax herself, her hand moving up to tentatively touch his silky fair hair. It felt just as good as she had thought it would, soft and springy to the touch, his face losing all trace of harshness in sleep.

With the back of the sofa on one side of her and Bart on the other, she felt coccooned in warmth, and soon drifted off to sleep herself. Some time during the night their positions shifted, Bart lying on his back, Eve's head resting on his chest as she curled up to him like a contented kitten.

She awoke with a start, looking down into caressing green eyes. 'Bart . . .!' she said achingly.

'I thought you would never wake up,' he groaned, rolling over so that she was beneath him, his thighs trapping her. 'You sleep very quietly.'

'You mean I don't snore?' She looked up at him teasingly.

'I mean you don't move about much. Perhaps that was as well in the circumstances,' he murmured, his gaze intent on her face. 'God, you look such a child,' he scowled.

Her hand moved up to touch the hardness of his cheek. 'I'm a woman, Bart.'

'Are you?'

'Oh yes,' she breathed softly.

'I hope so, because I'm going to kiss you anyway.' His head lowered and his firm, warm lips claimed hers, tilting her head back, making it difficult for her to breathe.

But she didn't care, her arms up around his back as she tried to be even closer to him. One of his hands moved to caress her thigh, moving slowly upward to cup her breast, and when she made no murmur of protest at this intimacy his thumb began to move rhythmically across the taut nipple that could easily be detected through the thin material of her shirt, the lacy bra no barrier at all.

She was unprepared for the wild surge of excitement that coursed through her body. No man, not even Carl, had given her pleasure like this. Pleasing her had been the last thing on Carl's mind that evening at the apartment, and when he made love to her all she had felt was pain as he allowed no respite for her innocence.

She hadn't even noticed the unfastening of her shirt, but she noticed Bart's probing fingers at the edge of her bra, the lacy material a flimsy barrier that he quickly dispensed with, lowering his head to her bared breasts, claiming one nipple between caressing lips and tongue.

After that she was lost, to the hard demand of his body, to her own answering response to that demand. Soon their bared torsos were fused together, their lips moving in a fevered kiss that seemed to have no end.

Finally Bart moved back with a gasp. 'You realise what's going to happen?' he groaned.

'Yes.' Her fingers ran tantalisingly down his rigid jaw.

He turned to kiss her palm, his eyes a deep glowing green. 'Do you mind?'

'No.' Her voice was husky.

'Then we aren't staying here.' He untangled his body from hers, taking her hand pulling her to her feet.

'Where are we going?' she demanded anxiously.

'To my room—or yours.' He looked down at her with passion-filled eyes. 'I really don't care which.'

'But—I—Maisie!' she reminded desperately.

Bart grinned down at her. 'Fast asleep hours ago. She looked in on us——'

'She did?'

'Mm,' he nodded. 'But she left again in a hurry.'

'Oh!' Her face was scarlet with embarrassment.

'Don't worry,' he placed a lingering kiss on her parted lips. 'Maisie may be outspoken, but she won't mention seeing us together.'

'But she'll know,' she cried as he dragged her up the stairs with him.

She instantly felt him tense. 'Do you mind?' he asked tersely.

'I—No,' she decided firmly. 'No, I don't mind.'

'Good girl.' He kissed her again. 'We'll go to my room, I have a shower.'

'Shower . . .?'

'Yes.' Bart grinned down at her. 'We're going to shower together, my little Eve. I'm going to wash you all over, and then you're going to wash me.'

She gulped. 'I am?'

'You are,' he chuckled at her flushed face. 'I love the way you blush. You're such a baby,' he teased.

She burrowed into his side as they entered his bedroom. 'You can say that—even after——'

'Forget him, Eve,' he rasped. 'Tonight think only of me. The past isn't going to matter between you and me.'

'We're just going to think of now?'

'Yes. And——'

'Oh, Bart,' she kissed him, thrilling with pleasure as she felt the desire surge through his body. 'I only want to think of now too.' She daren't think of tomorrow, knew that to think of losing Bart was something she *couldn't* think of yet.

Why should she think of the time she would be without him? She had him here and now, tonight. And maybe all the other nights until she had to leave here.

It wouldn't be enough, she knew that already, knew she would never have enough of Bart. But it was all she was going to be allowed, and strangely, with Bart, she could accept this temporary relationship. Just part of him was better than nothing.

He laid her down on the bed, making no effort to hide the naked desire in his eyes. Eve looked hastily away, seeing the huge double bed below her for the first time.

'You sleep—here?' It was the hugest bed she had ever seen, at least six feet across, and about eight feet long. She would be lost in a bed like this on her own. But she wasn't going to be alone, Bart would be with her, and not just for an hour or even two, but for the whole night, and as many other nights as she wanted to be with him.

Bart grinned. 'Yes, I sleep here. It gets a little lonely at times. But when I bought the bed I—well, I had plans.'

Pain darkened her eyes to navy blue. 'You—you were going to get married?'

'Don't look so surprised.' He sat down on the bed with her, gently touching her cheek. 'Don't you think I should be married?' he teased.

'I suppose so. But——'

'No more doubt, Eve,' he was suddenly serious, cupping each side of her face with his hands. 'Once you've shared this bed with me our relationship will be sealed. There'll be no turning back,' he warned.

'No . . .' She looked doubtful now, his talk of marrying some other woman reminding her that although she might love him, to him she would just be another woman to share his bed.

He sensed her uncertainty. 'Don't you want to?' he said gently.

She bit her lip. 'I thought I did, but——'

Bart stood up, pacing the room with forceful strides. 'You have to be sure,' he told her in a controlled voice. 'I'll be honest with you, Eve, I've wanted you from the moment I first saw you. But I can't make love to you until I know it's what you want too, not when I know how you suffered in the past. I never want you to turn around and say I seduced you into this. If we make love it has to be something we *both* want. You understand?' His piercing eyes seemed to look into her very soul.

'I—I understand.'

'And?' He waited, tensed.

'And I'm not sure.' She looked up at him with appealing eyes. 'I was, but I'm not now. I wish I could make you understand——'

'I do.' He pulled her to her feet. 'I can wait, Eve, until you're ready to come to me. Just knowing you're alive is enough for me.' His face darkened. 'I don't think I'll ever forget the horror of thinking you'd died in the mud and the rain,' he rasped, pulling her close to him.

Oh, what was the matter with her! This man had given her more during the few weeks she had known him than any other person she had ever known. She had him to thank for being alive, but more important than that, she had him to thank for giving her a purpose for *being* alive. She had been playing at life for the past five years, had fallen in with Derek's plans for her simply because she had nothing more important to do, had no plans or desires of her own.

But loving Bart had changed all that. Just being with him gave her a feeling of exhilaration, a thrill like nothing else had ever done. Why on earth was she hesitating about being made even more happy, about becoming his lover?

'I don't know why I hesitated, Bart,' she groaned, pressing herself against him. 'I'm just so grateful— Bart?' she questioned as he pushed her roughly away from him. 'What is it?'

His face was an angry mask, the lover of a few

minutes ago completely erased. 'I've had women make love with me for a lot of reasons, often mercenary ones,' he said harshly. 'But never, ever out of *gratitude*!'

'Oh no, you don't understand!' Eve put out her hands appealingly, 'I didn't mean that sort of gratitude. Bart, I——'

He rebuffed the touch of her hands, his mouth twisted in disgust. 'I would have done the same for anyone in trouble. Anyone, you understand!' he rasped. 'Is this the way it is with you, Eve? My God, you don't let a man take your body, take *you*, just because you're grateful to him!'

'Let me explain——'

'I've already heard enough. You'd better cover yourself,' he scorned.

Her cheeks blushed scarlet as she realised she had carried out the whole of the conversation with bared breasts, and Bart's mockery increased as she hastily covered her nakedness.

'Now take your gratitude and get out of my bedroom,' he ordered harshly, his expression bleak.

'Bart, please——'

'Get out, Eve, before I throw you out!'

She knew he meant it, knew he wasn't in the mood to listen to her. 'I—I'll see you in the morning?'

His mouth twisted. 'You may do.' He pointedly held the bedroom door open for her.

She crossed the short distance to her own room, all the while conscious of his angry eyes boring into her back. She turned at the door to make one last appeal. 'Bart——'

'Goodnight, Eve!' He slammed his door.

If only he would let her tell him she was grateful for being given the chance to love him, to finally know what loving really was.

CHAPTER EIGHT

SOME time towards morning she heard a bell ringing. In her half-dreaming state she dismissed it as a fire-engine or police car, her dreams suddenly taking on a frightening dimension, Bart seeming to be floating in and out of her subconscious, always angry, always accusing.

She woke with a start, the denial screaming on her lips. Bart! She had to see Bart, explain that she loved him, that being alive and able to love him was all she would ever want from him.

A light knock sounded on the door, and she sat up eagerly, the smile dimming a little as she saw it was Maisie.

'I didn't mean to wake you,' Maisie said regretfully. 'But it's after eleven, and there's a Mr James on the telephone for you. I asked him to call back later, but he said he wasn't able to.'

Eve gathered her scattered wits together. It was after *eleven*! Goodness, she had almost slept the day away. And Derek was waiting to talk to her on the telephone. 'Tell him I'll be right there,' she scrambled out of bed, hurrying to the wardrobe to take out white cotton trousers and a blue blouse.

'Now just calm down,' Maisie tutted. 'Take things easy. I'm sure this Mr James can wait a minute or two while you dress yourself.'

Eve slowed down her movements as Maisie left to tell Derek she wouldn't be long. What could Derek be telephoning her about?

He was bubbling over with excitement when she

finally got downstairs to take his call. 'You could have been a bit quicker,' he chided impatiently.

'Sorry,' she mumbled, still trying to wake up.

'I just wanted to let you know I have to take a rain-check on my visits to you. I have to get a flight out tomorrow. Tomorrow, Eve! Can you believe it?'

As she didn't know what he was talking about, no. 'What flight?' she asked dazedly.

'The one to New York. Halstead telephoned me this morning. He actually telephoned me himself, Eve. And he wants me out there tomorrow,' he told her ex-citedly.

'Derek——'

'You don't have any idea what I'm talking about, do you?' he said impatiently.

'No,' she admitted softly.

'God, you sound awful! What have you been doing?'

'Sleeping!' she snapped. 'I am here to rest, you know.'

'Okay,' he sighed. 'But didn't Bart tell you about this job in New York?'

'Bart?' Eve frowned. 'What does he have to do with all this?'

'Everything!' The excitement returned to Derek's voice. 'He made all the initial arrangements.'

'For what?'

'For me to work in a recording studio in New York!'

'He—he did?' Her hand clutched the telephone.

'Isn't it great?' Derek enthused. 'It's something I've always been interested in. Of course I've got to start at the bottom and learn everything, but it's still going to be exciting. And Bart's brother-in-law——'

'His brother-in-law?' she repeated dazedly, feeling as if everything were moving too fast for her.

'For goodness' sake wake up, Eve. You don't seem to be taking this in at all.'

'Then explain what you're talking about!' She lost her temper with him.

'Bart's brother-in-law is David Halstead. You have heard of him, haven't you?'

'Of course,' Eve confirmed dryly at his derisive tone. Everyone had heard of the famous American record producer.

'Bart made some enquiries about my going out there to work for him. And this morning he called me, David Halstead himself, to invite me over.'

That Derek was suffering from a case of hero-worship was obvious. 'It's all a bit sudden, isn't it, Derek?'

'Of course it isn't,' he snapped. 'It's been in the planning for weeks.'

'How many weeks?' she asked suspiciously.

'A couple. Ever since I lost your contract to Bart, actually. I was at a bit of a loose end——'

'And so Bart decided to tie it,' she finished tauntingly. 'My, how he loves to organise other people's lives for them!'

'Eve——'

'I'm sorry, Derek,' she sighed, putting a hand up to her wayward hair. 'I never wake up in a good mood, you know that. I really hope you get on well in America,' she added sincerely.

'Thanks. I'll have to go now, there's so much to do. But I'll call you from New York.'

'Fine,' she acknowledged. 'Say goodbye to Judy for me.'

' 'Bye, Eve.' He hung up.

She slowly replaced her own receiver, suddenly feeling very lost and alone. She had no one now that Derek and Judy were gone, her aunt and uncle were not expected back for some weeks yet. But she had Bart! Or at least, she would have, if she could just make him understand that her gratitude wasn't for saving her life but for giving her a reason to live it.

'All right?' Maisie enquired as Eve wandered into the kitchen.

She looked up, startled, having been deep in thought. 'I—Oh yes. Just a friend letting me know he was leaving the country.'

Maisie nodded. 'As long as it didn't upset you.'

Eve blushed as she remembered Bart saying Maisie had seen them together in the study last night. 'No, he—he didn't upset me,' she gave a nervy smile. 'What are you making?' she asked interestedly, hoping Maisie wouldn't guess the reason for her blushes.

'Cheese soufflé for your lunch,' the other woman said with satisfaction. 'It's Adam's favourite. He can have some when he gets back.'

If Adam was out then that meant Bart was out too. She hadn't expected him to be at work this morning. 'Will Adam be back soon?' she asked casually, her real interest in Bart's return.

'Not long now,' Maisie assured her.

Eve nodded, tingling with the anticipation of seeing Bart again. 'I think I'll just go and finish my wash.'

'Take this with you.' Maisie poured her a cup of coffee and handed it to her.

'Thanks,' she smiled gratefully.

It didn't take her long to wash and tidy her appearance. She added a light make-up, remembering that Bart disliked the heavy make-up she wore on stage as much as she did. Her eyes glowed, and there was a slight flush to her cheeks. She looked like a woman in love, and surely Bart would see that when he returned.

Maisie had put the soufflé in the oven when she rejoined her, and the two of them sat down to enjoy a cup of coffee together. Eve refused any idea of food.

The lunch would be ready soon enough. Besides, she was too keyed up to eat at the moment.

'I hope Adam wasn't offended by my hurried departure last night.' She knew the subject had to be brought up, much as it embarrassed her.

'He wasn't offended at all,' his mother dismissed. 'He understands that you're here to be with Bart——'

'Oh, but I'm not! I mean——' Eve blushed uncomfortably as she realised how ridiculous her denial must sound in the light of what Maisie had seen last night. 'It isn't like that, Maisie,' she said lamely.

'So Bart told me before he left this morning. In a fine old temper he was too.' She eyed Eve questioningly, knowing she must have something to do with his bad mood.

'Like you said, he's tired and overworked,' Eve evaded.

'That he is, and sleepless nights don't help either.'

'Sleepless——? Oh, I'm sure he slept, Maisie.' For a couple of hours at least! After the way they had parted she wasn't so sure about later, but earlier in the study he had slept soundlessly.

The housekeeper stood up to remove their empty cups. 'Not when he's woken up by noisy telephone calls in the middle of the night he doesn't,' she tutted her disapproval, whether just of late night calls or of telephones in general Eve wasn't sure.

She frowned her puzzlement. 'Bart had a telephone call during the night?' It would explain the ringing she had heard.

'From Australia!' Maisie snorted. 'No respect for people trying to sleep.'

'I don't suppose they realised——'

'Oh, they realised all right. But it was urgent, they said. So urgent that Bart's had to go rushing over there this morning.'

Eve felt as if all the colour had left her cheeks. 'Bart's in Australia?' she asked weakly.

'Well, not yet he isn't,' Maisie teased. 'But he will be. And I pity whoever is waiting for him at the other end, his temper isn't likely to have been improved by that long flight. He hates flying at the best of times, says it bores him to death.'

Eve could imagine that such a dynamic man would find lengthy inactivity rather irksome. But all she could think of at that moment was that she wouldn't be able to talk to Bart after all, to tell him she loved him.

'I—Do you have any idea when he'll be back?'

Maisie shook her head. 'I doubt he knows himself. If he could have got hold of Sean Stevens this morning I think he would have wrung his neck.'

That sounded like Bart. 'His ex-assistant had something to do with Bart having to leave so suddenly?'

'Been up to his tricks over there too. Bart put him in charge over there for three months last year. They've just discovered his fiddling of the books.'

Embezzling, Bart had called it, but she realised Maisie was too down-to-earth to call it anything but what it was. 'So he could be gone for weeks?' she said in dismay.

'I really have no idea,' she was told regretfully. 'He did say he would call you, though,' Maisie added encouragingly.

'He did?' Eve's expression brightened.

'Mm. But he didn't say when.'

'Oh.'

'I'm really sorry, dear,' Maisie sympathised. 'But I'm sure he'll call you soon.'

She didn't expect a call that night, he wouldn't even have arrived yet, let alone thought about telephoning her. She barely slept, wishing the hours away until morning. Bart wouldn't call here when he knew it was night-time.

He didn't call the next day either, or the day after that, his call finally coming on the third day, three days when Eve had lived only for the ringing of the telephone.

And she had to go and miss his call when it finally came! Maisie had been trying to persuade her to let Adam at least take her out for a drive, but she kept refusing. Until the day of Bart's telephone call! She had been so depressed with staying in all the time, frightened to move away from the telephone, that when Adam suggested driving her to the coast she had readily agreed.

She felt like crying when she returned and Maisie told her Bart had called while she was out. The day hadn't been a success anyway. Heavy rain prevented her from going on to the beach, and missing talking to Bart just about finished her.

Her eyes filled with tears before she turned hastily away and ran up the stairs to her bedroom.

'Come on, now,' Maisie gently chided as she came into the room, sitting down beside Eve's prone body on the bed. 'He'll call again, I'm sure of it.'

Eve looked up with tear-drenched eyes. 'Do you really think so?' she sniffed.

'Yes, really. Here,' Maisie handed her a tissue. 'Now come down and eat your dinner, or I'll be in trouble when Bart gets back. You look worse now than when he first brought you here.'

She knew that, but she was missing Bart so much she didn't feel like eating, and at night she just couldn't sleep. If only they hadn't parted so disastrously! If only she had told him that night that she loved him. There seemed to be a lot of 'ifs' in her life at the moment.

She went down to the kitchen with Maisie, having

taken to spending most of her time in there with the older woman. 'Did he mention me at all?' she asked tentatively.

'Well, he asked for you, and when I said you were out——'

'Did you tell him I'd gone out with Adam?' Eve asked in dismay.

'Well, of course, dear. He wouldn't like to think I'd let you go wandering off on your own.'

He wouldn't like to think she had been out with Adam either, his behaviour the night he had found her playing cards in the kitchen with the other man telling her that much.

'Does he know when he's coming back yet?' She couldn't keep the eagerness out of her voice. It was too late for pretence where Maisie was concerned, she had given away her love for Bart a hundred different ways the last few days, but especially the night Maisie had found her sleeping on the sofa in Bart's study. She felt close to him there, could relive their intimacy, could almost imagine he was there with her. Almost . . .

'Another couple of days, he thinks,' the housekeeper told her now.

Her pulse quickened. 'So he could be back at the weekend?'

'Let's hope so, hmm,' Maisie said gently.

She did hope, it was the only thing that kept her going the next few days. Then on Friday evening Bart telephoned again. Eve was in the bath, but she quickly got out of the scented water when Maisie told her Bart was on the telephone wanting to talk to her.

'Hello,' she said huskily, her heart pounding so loud she thought he must be able to hear it.

'You sound breathless.' His voice sounded clear, making him seem very near. If only he was! 'You didn't run down the stairs, did you?' his tone was disapproving. 'Maisie said you were in your room.'

'I was in the bath,' she corrected. 'And now I'm— I'm in your bedroom.'

There was a lengthy silence. 'Are you sitting on my bed?' he asked at last.

'Yes. But don't worry, I'm dry——'

'I couldn't give a damn if you were soaking wet,' he dismissed tersely. 'God, it's good to talk to you,' he groaned suddenly.

'You too,' she said huskily.

'Did you enjoy your day out with Adam?'

He hadn't liked it, she had known he wouldn't. 'I didn't go *with* Adam,' she told him firmly. 'He just drove me. I waited and waited for your call.' Her voice broke emotionally.

'Eve?' Bart queried sharply. 'Eve, are you crying?'

'No! Yes! Yes,' she admitted softly as fresh tears cascaded down her cheeks.

'For God's sake, *why?*' he groaned.

'Because I miss you,' Eve told him huskily.

'If it's any consolation, I've missed you too.'

'You have?'

He gave a husky laugh. 'Well, don't sound surprised! The way you left me the other night I haven't been able to get you out of my mind.'

'Bart, about the other night——'

'Not on the phone, Eve,' his voice was suddenly terse.

'But I want to explain——'

'And you can, when I get home.'

'When will that be?' she asked eagerly.

'The next couple of days. I'll call Adam from the airport when to come and pick me up.'

'I'll come with him,' she said instantly.

He drew a ragged breath. 'Eve, don't start something you can't finish,' he sighed.

'But I can!' She blushed. 'I mean——'

Bart gave a husky laugh. 'Yes, what did you mean?'

'I mean that you misunderstood me the other night.' Oh, she couldn't tell him she loved him over the telephone! But she could do the next best thing! 'I mean that I'm going to sleep in this bed tonight,' she said firmly. 'And every other night until you no longer want me.'

'Eve!' he groaned.

'I mean it, Bart,' she told him strongly.

'I really think you do.' There was wonder in his voice.

'I do.'

'God, you pick the damnedest times . . .! I'm thousands of miles away, Eve, and you can still arouse me.'

She blushed at the intimacy of his words, but her determination wasn't diminished. Bart had once told her that if she ever wanted him to kiss her again she was going to have to ask. Well, she wanted more than kisses, and she was no longer afraid to say so.

'Then just think how much better it will be when you get home,' she encouraged softly.

'I'm thinking. God, we can't make love over the telephone!' he moaned.

Eve gave a breathless laugh. 'We aren't doing so badly!' Except that she ached for the flesh-and-blood man beside her. And she knew that he felt the same. Bart was a man who was ultimately honest about his feelings, and the only way to reach him was with the same honesty. 'Do you sleep on either side of the bed or just in the middle?'

'The middle. Why?' he sounded puzzled by the question.

'Because I want to sleep where you sleep. That way I can feel closer to you.'

'Eve, I have to get off this phone!' he said in a strangulated voice. 'Just hold that mood until I get home.'

'I will,' she promised huskily. 'And it isn't a mood, Bart, it's the way I feel about you.'

'Eve—Look, I have to go now.' His voice was suddenly brisk, telling her that wherever he was he was no longer alone. 'Keep the bed warm for me,' he added in a lowered voice. 'I'll be back as soon as I can.'

She must have floated back to her own room, and was towelling her hair dry when Maisie limped into the room. She had learnt from talking to the other woman that her hip had been damaged during the war. It didn't seem to give her any pain, she just had the permanent limp.

'Everything all right now?' She viewed Eve's sparkling eyes and glowing cheeks with a knowing smile.

'Everything is—wonderful,' Eve confirmed, standing up to dance lightly around the room.

'And is Bart in the same state of euphoria?' Maisie asked dryly.

She flushed with pleasure. 'I think so.'

'Dare I ask when he's coming home?'

'Soon. Very soon.'

Maisie nodded, as if she had expected it. 'I knew he loved you as soon as I saw the two of you together.'

Eve bit her lip, shaking her head. 'I—He—No, he doesn't love me, Maisie.'

'Don't be silly, of course he does.'

Maybe it would be better to let Maisie believe that. After all, Maisie was going to be here long after she, Eve, had gone from Bart's life.

'Maybe,' she agreed lightly.

'Are you going to eat some dinner now? You haven't been eating enough to keep a bird alive,' Maisie scolded.

'Tonight you can prepare me a banquet!' Eve gave a glowing smile.

'I'll do my best,' the other woman laughed, obviously relieved at seeing her so happy.

She spent the night in Bart's bed as she had promised him she would, burying her face in the pillows to breathe in his aftershave. For the first time in nights she slept well, although she managed to make the bed and get back to her own room before Maisie brought up her morning tea. Maisie would have to know of her relationship with Bart sooner or later, but she would rather Bart were here when it happened.

No word came from Bart that day, although she did have a call from Derek. Apparently he and David Halstead were coming over from New York for a few days, and he intended visiting her while he was here.

'Is Bart's sister coming over too?' she asked interestedly.

'Not that I know of. But she could be. David may have taken me under his wing, at Bart's request, I think, but he certainly doesn't confide his private life to me.'

'I'd better tell Bart just in case.' He might want her out of the way if a member of his family was coming to visit.

'How are you getting on with him now? Still hating his guts?' She could hear the smile in Derek's voice.

'Just the opposite,' she told him lightly, smiling herself when she heard his gasp of surprise.

'You *love* him?'

Eve gave a happy laugh. 'Yes.'

'Good God!'

'Don't tell me you're speechless, Derek?' she teased.

'Just about,' he admitted. 'Look, I have to get on now, but you can tell me all about this sudden change of feeling when I get back to England. Just wait until I tell Judy!' came his dazed parting comment.

Bart didn't call that evening either, but she once

again spent the night in his bed, just longing for the time he would share it with her.

Maisie was busy making scones for tea when Eve came down for breakfast. 'Bart's favourite,' she looked up to explain.

Eve's pulse quickened, her breath suddenly catching in her throat. 'Does that mean—Is he——' She was so excited she couldn't speak.

'He's already home,' Maisie answered her unfinished questions. 'At least, he should be in about half an hour.'

Eve frowned, her excitement slowly fading. 'Half an hour?'

Maisie nodded. 'Adam's gone to pick him up from the airport.'

'Oh no!' she groaned. 'I wanted to go with him,' she explained at the other woman's questioning look. 'I told Bart I would.'

'Well, there's no need to get yourself into a state about it. Bart will understand.'

But would he? Meeting him at the airport was supposed to have been the start of their relationship. When she didn't turn up with Adam he would think she had changed her mind and that this was her way of telling him.

One look at his face when he got home was enough to tell her that was exactly what he did think; the shutters were firmly down over his luminous green eyes, his mouth a thin, uncompromising line.

'It's good to have you back!' Maisie gave him an affectionate hug, undeterred by his grimness.

Eve wished she had the nerve to act so spontaneously, but the chill in Bart's eyes as he looked over Maisie's head at her seemed to freeze her to the spot.

She ran clammy palms down her denim-clad thighs. 'Welcome home, Bart,' she greeted nervously.

'Eve,' he gave her an abrupt nod of acknowledgment.

'You—you're looking well.'

'I wish the same could be said for you.' His gaze flickered disapprovingly over her too-slender curves. 'You're thinner than ever.'

She flushed. 'I——'

'Now don't go starting on the girl as soon as you get home,' Maisie rushed to her defence. 'She's been eating really well the last couple of days.'

'Really?' Bart's expression didn't alter. 'It doesn't look like it,' he said dismissively.

Eve flinched. This wasn't going at all as she had planned it, Bart's cruelty instantly brought tears into her eyes.

He frowned at the shimmering tears. 'Maybe I should get Edgar out to take a look at you.'

'Get who you want!' she choked. 'I won't see them!' She ran blindly up the stairs.

'Now look what you've done!' she could hear Maisie scold. 'And she's been so looking forward to your coming home.'

Eve turned at the top of the stairs, looking down to find both Maisie and Bart staring back at her, Maisie with concern, Bart with an anger he didn't attempt to hide.

'I wish he'd never come home,' she shouted. 'Never!' She turned and slammed into her bedroom.

The pounding feet on the stairs warned her of Bart's coming before he exploded into the room, his face a livid, angry mask. Eve cringed back on the bed, frightened of his white-hot anger as he slammed the door behind him.

'I came home,' he ground out fiercely, 'because this *is* my home. Have you forgotten that?'

'No . . .'

'I should damn well think not,' he snapped, his eyes blazing. 'And don't you ever order me out of it again.'

'Oh, I—I didn't——'

'Yes, you did, damn you!' He came over to kneel on the bed, grasping her shoulders to shake her roughly. 'If anyone leaves here it will be you. Do you understand?'

Shaking her caused fresh tears to cascade down her cheeks, but he seemed immune to them. 'When do you want me to go?' she quavered.

'Now!' He flung her viciously back down onto the bed, his mouth twisted contemptuously. 'Just pack your things and get out. It can't be soon enough for me.'

'I—Bart——'

'Get out, Eve!' he shouted before slamming back out of the bedroom.

Eve sobbed uncontrollably for several minutes, then she stood up to open the wardrobe and begin packing.

CHAPTER NINE

SHE was still packing when Maisie came quietly into the room a few minutes later. Eve glanced at her, but she was too miserable to even attempt to make conversation.

'What are you doing, child?' Maisie watched her agitated movements.

'Packing,' she stated the obvious.

'But why?'

Once again Eve glanced up. 'Because Bart told me to, because he no longer wants me here.'

Maisie frowned. 'Did he say that?'

'Oh yes,' she gave a choked laugh, 'he made his feeling more than clear.'

The other woman sighed. 'He didn't mean it,' she said gently. 'He's tired, and when you're tired you tend to say and do things you don't mean.'

'Not Bart,' Eve shook her head. 'He always means what he says.'

'He doesn't want you to go, you know he doesn't. Why, only yesterday you were over the moon because you were both in love and thinking of getting married.'

'No, Maisie,' she said firmly. 'Bart's offer to me has never involved marriage.'

An embarrassed flush coloured the older woman's cheeks. 'You mean he—he—Bart offered to make you his mistress?'

'Yes,' she sighed.

'I don't believe it!'

Eve shrugged. 'You only have to ask him.'

'He's gone to bed, he's tired after the flight.'

And when he woke up she would be gone! 'Then ask him later.' She closed her suitcase. 'You've been very kind to me, Maisie,' she smiled wanly. 'I've appreciated it.'

The other woman's expression softened. 'You're easy to be kind to. Where do you intend going?'

She shrugged. 'Probably to a hotel to start with. Then I'll——'

'We'll see about that!' Maisie was suddenly angry. 'We'll see about this mistress business too. I've never heard the like!' she snorted disgustedly. 'You're not to go anywhere until I've spoken to Bart.'

'Oh, but——'

'Promise me, Eve,' she said sternly.

If the truth were known she was feeling rather weary after throwing all her belongings into her suitcase; a few minutes' sit-down while Bart confirmed his wish for her to leave wouldn't be a bad idea.

'All right,' she sat down heavily. 'But it won't do any good.'

'We'll see about that,' Maisie repeated before leaving the room, a determined set to her mouth.

Eve could hear the murmur of voices across the corridor, and then Bart's bedroom door closed, the voices less distinct now.

Dear Maisie, she was like a mother hen defending her chick. It was nice to feel protected like this, although she was still certain of the outcome of the conversation.

She was lying down on the bed when Bart came into the room a few minutes later, Maisie nowhere to be seen. Eve sat up, instantly on the defensive.

'I didn't ask Maisie to come and see you. I——'

'I know you didn't.' He was calm now, his temper all gone. He had showered since she had last seen him, his hair still damp, a black towelling robe his only clothing as far as she could see, his legs bare from his thighs to his feet. 'But I'm glad she did,' he added softly. 'What's all this about my intending installing you here as my mistress?'

'Oh, I didn't say it would be here——'

'But you did think I intended making you my mistress?' he queried softly.

'I—Well—Yes.' She eyed him apprehensively, sure that this calm could only precede the storm.

'Are you aware of the fact that Maisie has just handed in her notice?' he asked dryly.

Eve went pale. 'Oh no!' she gasped. 'I—She can't do that!'

'She just did.'

'Well, I—You—You seem to be taking it calmly!' She was outraged at his callousness. 'Maisie has been with you for years,' she stormed, her eyes sparkling angrily. 'You can't let her leave!'

'I don't intend to.'

'Oh, you mean you persuaded her to stay,' she sighed her relief, glad not to have caused Maisie to leave the place she loved so much.

'I not only did that,' his mouth quirked, 'I gave her a raise.'

Eve stood up to clear her things from the dressing-table, having missed them earlier. 'I'm sure she deserves one.' Bart stood in front of her reaching one of her bottles of perfume. 'Would you mind?' she asked stiltedly, staring at the knotted belt of his robe.

'Yes, I would,' his voice was soft. 'I would mind very much. Why didn't you tell me you didn't even know about my call from the airport?' He gently lifted her chin, his green-eyed gaze easily holding hers. 'Why?' he repeated.

She was trembling from his touch, unable to hold

back her instant response to him. 'You didn't exactly give me a chance to,' she reminded him.

He pulled her close against him, his arms going about her. 'No, I didn't did I?' he derided. 'I'm sorry, Eve. I was an absolute swine to you when I got back just now.'

'You were.' She burrowed against his hair-roughened chest, loving the clean male smell of him.

His chest rumbled with laughter. 'My honest little Eve!' His hand caressed her hair as he held her head against him. 'But we haven't been completely honest with each other, have we?' he said softly. 'Not about our feelings, anyway. Eve, the other night, the night I took you to my room, I told you that once you'd slept with me our relationship would be sealed. What did you think I meant by that remark?'

'Well, that I—that we——'

'That we would continue to sleep together,' he finished for her.

'Yes,' she mumbled.

'Oh, Eve, Eve!' he chided, leaning back against the dressing-table, taking her with him, holding her in between his splayed legs as he looked down at her with gentle eyes. 'I didn't mean that at all, I meant that once I'd taken you, made love to you, I wouldn't be able to let you go. Not ever. I want to marry you, Eve.'

She looked up with a gulp. 'M—Marry me . . .?'

'Don't look so shocked,' he spluttered with laughter, suddenly sobering. 'Or does the idea of marriage to me not appeal to you?' he asked anxiously.

'Oh yes! I mean——'

'No, don't spoil it.' His arms tightened about her, his mouth nuzzling her throat. 'God, if you knew how much I want you for my wife,' he groaned. 'I've thought of nothing else but marrying you for the last six months.'

'Six months?' Eve frowned up at him.

Bart nodded. 'That was when I first saw you. You were a guest on one of those up-and-coming star shows, singing your last record, the one that reached the bottom of the charts. I took one look at you and—God, I love you, Eve. I love you so damned much!'

She couldn't believe what he was saying. He couldn't love her, not really.

He seemed to sense her withdrawal, looking down at her with concerned eyes. 'You don't love me——'

'Oh, but I do!' she contradicted. 'I tried to tell you the other night——'

'You told me you were grateful,' he recalled bitterly.

'Not in that way,' she sighed. 'I wanted to explain, but you wouldn't listen. You—you told me to get out.'

Bart gave a rueful smile. 'It seems to be a habit with me lately.' His eyes darkened. 'But if you weren't grateful because I was the one who found you lying by the river just why were you grateful?'

She explained to him exactly what she meant, watching the hope lighting his eyes.

'The time we've wasted!' he groaned. He shook his head. 'When you weren't at the airport as you had said you would be I thought you'd changed your mind. I'd thought of nothing but you ever since that telephone call, and my disappointment when you weren't at Heathrow——! Well, you saw what I was like,' he said ruefully. 'Bloody cruel. But you really are too thin, my darling,' he frowned his concern.

'I've been pining for you.'

He looked at her uncertainly. 'Eve?' His query was almost tentative.

She looked at him fearlessly. 'I have, Bart. I—I love you too, you see. I didn't mean to but—well, suddenly I did!'

He laughed at her woebegone expression. 'That's hardly the way to tell a man you love him,' he chided.

Eve flushed. 'I'm sorry. I didn't mean—I just wanted to explain——'

'It doesn't matter.' He pulled her towards him. 'You can show me instead.'

'Sh—show you?'

His hand moved up to gently caress her cheek. 'You're still shy with me,' he said wonderingly. 'I just want you to kiss me, Eve. I've hungered for you the last few days, needed you so badly. It was no way to send a man off on business.'

She looked up at him shyly. 'I have a much better way of welcoming you back.'

His eyebrows rose teasingly. 'You do?'

'Mm.'

'Go ahead,' he invited eagerly.

She raised her lips to his, revelling in her right to be able to kiss him whenever she wanted to. And right now she wanted to very badly.

And Bart was letting her do the kissing, responding passionately, but letting her be the one in control. She put her hands on his chest beneath the robe, loving the silky texture of his skin, her lips following a similar path as she felt him shudder beneath her.

'I love you, Bart,' she whispered huskily against his skin.

His arms tightened around her. 'You'd better,' he groaned.

'I do.' Her hands moved to the belt on his robe, easily untying its single fastening, parting the robe to move against his naked body. 'Oh, Bart——'

'For God's sake kiss me!' he moaned heatedly.

He was the master now, the feel of his lips moving fiercely over hers making her feel weak with desire, deepening the kiss to intimacy.

'Oh yes, Bart,' she eagerly accepted his show of passion. 'I want you too.'

'Yes,' he murmured, not triumphantly or mockingly, just a simple acknowledgement of their mutual desire. 'You're coming with me.' He tied his robe loosely, swinging her up in his arms to carry her through to his bedroom, laying her tenderly down before he began to undress her.

She watched his face as he slowly removed each item of clothing, saw the pleasure it gave him to look at her nakedness, his firm brown hands lingering on her creamy white breasts.

'I knew you would look right in this bed.' His eyes seemed to be on fire, his hand trembling as it moved down the silkiness of her thigh.

Eve licked her lips nervously. 'The woman you were going to marry——'

'What woman?' he queried vaguely, his lips against her breast.

'The one you bought the bed for.'

'You,' he said huskily.

Her eyes widened. 'Me?'

Bart raised his head, looking at her teasingly. 'Are we going to talk or make love?'

She flushed. 'Well, I—Can't we do both?'

He laughed softly, taking off his robe to lie down beside her and pull the covers over them both, his arm cradling her against his chest. 'We can, but not that sort of talk.'

'Then I'd rather make love,' she told him huskily.

His eyes gleamed down at her teasingly. 'I have no intention of making love to you until we're married.'

'You haven't?' she gasped.

'No,' he shook his head. 'I love you, I want you for my wife, I'm not in such a rush that I can't wait—oh, three or four days for you.'

Eve gave a happy laugh. 'What a sacrifice!'

'It is, young lady.' He looked down at her with a mock stern expression. 'My body aches for you,' he told her deeply.

She blushed, burying her face against his chest. 'But if you don't want to make love to me,' she looked up at him, 'what am I doing here in this bed with you?'

'Telling me in more than words that you love me,' he said seriously. 'I know how much you hate the idea of a physical relationship with a man——'

'Not with you,' she assured him. 'Never with you.'

He kissed her hard on the mouth. 'That's how I know that you truly love me. And I did buy this bed for you, although now that we're both in it it seems a little on the large side.' He frowned. 'I could lose you in here. Maybe I should change it for a single,' he added wolfishly.

'And what would Maisie think of that?' She played with the dark blond hair on his chest.

'Maisie already knows exactly how I feel about you. She had much more perception than you, as she guessed the day I brought you here.'

'You weren't exactly encouraging.'

'And why should I have been? I told you what to do if you wanted my kisses.'

'Ask for them.' She grimaced. 'You knew I couldn't do that.'

His eyes twinkled down at her. 'You didn't do so badly that night in my study.'

'I——'

'You wanted me that night,' he told her firmly. 'And that offer to massage my neck was your way of telling me so.'

'I—Yes,' she admitted quietly.

His arms tightened about her. 'I've had a hard battle

to win you, Eve, but now that I have, I don't ever intend to let you go.'

'I don't want to go anywhere without you.'

'Don't worry, you won't.'

She looked up at him, seeing the lines of tiredness that he was trying to fight off. 'Maybe I should leave now.'

His expression darkened. 'I was in a temper when I told you to leave—I didn't mean it.'

She leant up on one elbow to gently smoothe his brow. 'I didn't mean leave the house, darling,' she soothed. 'Maisie said you're tired, I thought I would go and let you get some sleep.'

'I'll sleep much more comfortably with you here.' He pushed her gently down on the bed. 'The night I slept in your arms was the best night's sleep I've ever had. I've fantasised about repeating the experience ever since.' He laid his head against her.

How he could even think of sleep when she could only think of how close their naked bodies were she just didn't know. Maybe it was different for men, maybe——

'I want you just as badly,' he murmured suddenly. 'But I want our marriage to start off the right way.'

'How did you know——'

'Your heart is beating so fast it's deafening me.' He looked up at her, smiling softly. 'When I make love to you for the first time it isn't going to be where Maisie can come barging into the room at any time. You may have noticed she has no qualms about doing exactly that.'

'I'll never be able to thank her enough for sorting out the tangle we'd got ourselves into,' said Eve.

Bart grinned. 'I told her she can be godmother to our first child.'

'Oh!' she blushed prettily.

'Do you want children?' he asked seriously.

'As long as they all promise to have blond hair and green eyes,' she said shyly.

'Strange, I had visions of black hair and blue eyes.'

Eve laughed. 'If they're as contrary as we are they'll probably have red hair and brown eyes!'

'You could be right,' Bart agreed ruefully. 'Now let me get some sleep, woman. I have a lot of things to arrange later today.'

'You aren't going to work?' Her tone showed her disappointment.

'No, I'm not. I'm going to see if I can buy a deserted island somewhere where we can be alone for three months. You think I'm joking, don't you?' he kissed her lightly on the nose. 'Believe me, three months alone with you isn't anywhere near long enough for me to show you all the different ways I love you.'

Her cheeks were flushed, her eyes glowing as she felt completely cocooned by Bart's love for her. 'When will we be married?'

'As soon as I can arrange it. Before the end of the week, definitely. Now let me get some sleep and start building up my strength.' He grinned at her shy embarrassment. 'Maybe you'd better do the same,' he teased. 'You won't be sleeping much in future either. And you won't be working. Contrary to what you thought, about my wanting to get you back out to work, I don't approve of my wife working.'

'If you decided to marry me six months ago——'

'I did,' he told her firmly.

'Why did you finance my concerts?'

'Because you had to see if you could do it. You have a fantastic voice, Eve, very sexy, and I don't mind if you want to keep making records, but I won't have you wearing yourself out doing concerts. Besides,' his arms tightened, 'I couldn't bear to let you leave me for weeks at a time.'

'I wouldn't want to go. Derek and I have already decided I'm not cut out for that type of career.'

Bart gave a wolfish grin. 'And as your new business manager I know exactly what career you are cut out for. Being my wife is going to be a full-time job.'

She touched his hair lovingly. 'I hope so.'

'It will be,' he promised sleepily. 'Now are you ever going to stop talking, woman?' he growled.

She snuggled against him comfortably. 'Yes, Bart.'

He rolled over on his back with a groan. 'I'm not sure I can sleep now. I want you too badly to just be able to lie here next to you and not make love to you.'

'You don't have to.' She touched him tentatively.

'Yes, I do,' he said firmly. 'You're never going to be able to say I took advantage of you.'

Eve sensuously touched the tip of her tongue to her top lip, seeing Bart's eyes darken as he watched the movement. 'How about,' she said slowly, 'if I . . . take advantage of *you*?'

For a moment his eyes widened in surprise, then a slow smile spread across his flushed, handsome features. 'Well, that's something else completely,' he murmured invitingly.

She was only too happy to take up that invitation. 'I thought it might be,' she laughed throatily. 'But wouldn't you rather go to sleep?' she said with feigned innocence. 'I thought you were tired.'

He moved so quickly that before she was hardly aware of it he was lying on top of her, his eyes dark with the passion his body couldn't conceal. 'Stop tormenting me, Eve,' he groaned, his mouth taking fierce possession of hers.

What happened next was a complete revelation to Eve, as Bart threw off the bedclothes and began to kiss and touch every inch of her body. When he became too intimate she tried to stop him, pulling his head back up to her lips, but Bart was stronger than she was, and he was determined to know all of her.

When his body finally joined hers she knew a moment's pain, and then a lifetime of ecstasy, Bart taking her to the very pinnacle of desire, as shattered as she was when they finally floated back to earth.

Eve placed featherlight kisses all over his chest, just wanting to touch and kiss him, to keep this closeness for ever.

His hand was shaking as it moved up to caress her flushed face. 'Eve . . .' he seemed to be having difficulty finding the words. 'Eve, just now—I'd swear——'

'Yes?' Her bubble of happiness seemed to burst as he continued to frown. 'What is it? Did—did I do something wrong?'

His expression instantly gentled. 'Of course you didn't. You were beautiful, you're always beautiful. But the pleasure—I'd swear you'd never known the pleasure before. Your eyes widened with shock just before, and—My God, what did that man do to you, Eve?' he demanded tautly.

She sighed, unable to meet his piercing green eyes. 'You're right, I was shocked. I'd never realised . . . You see, he—he lost his temper, and—and——'

'Raped you?' Bart was white with fury. 'Did he rape you, Eve?' He shook her.

'I—No, not exactly. It was my own fault. I told you I was naïve.' She gave a bitter laugh. 'Just how naïve I didn't realise until he decided to turn up at my apartment as if he owned me. You see, he found me the apartment. I didn't know—I had no idea——' She sighed, biting her lip.

'So that's why you were so bitter about my setting you up in an apartment,' Bart said slowly. 'I've never done that, Eve. I've never humiliated any woman in that way.'

'Maisie told me you never stay in London.'

He smoothed the damp hair back from her brow.
'That isn't exactly true,' he told her gently. 'There
have been women . . .'

'Well, of course there have,' she instantly defended.
'Otherwise you wouldn't make love so beautifully. But
none of them was your wife.'

'No, you can't add that to my sins. And do I make
love beautifully?' he teased to ease the tension.

'Oh yes!' The smile she gave him was dazzling.

He groaned in his throat, at once kissing her again,
desire rekindling. 'This may be ungentlemanly of me,'
he raised his head with effort, 'but unless I kick you
out of bed I'm going to make love to you again—and
the first of those contrary kids may come along
before we want them to.' He laughed as the colour
flooded her cheeks. 'You hadn't thought of that, had
you?'

'No . . .' The thought hadn't even crossed her mind.
'But I wouldn't mind,' she told him calmly.

'Neither would I,' he chuckled. 'But I don't intend
loaning this body out to my child for at least another
year or so. I have other uses for it.'

She was learning to withstand the intimacy of his
teasing now, although she still blushed. 'Only for a
year?' she pouted, indulging in some teasing of her
own.

'No, you little wildcat—He called you that, didn't
he?' Bart pounced as she paled.

'Yes,' she groaned, turning her face away. 'Although
it was never true with him, not the way you mean it.'

'I know that.' Bart held her chin and forced her to
look at him. 'You never have to be ashamed of what
happened to you,' he told her gently. 'As far as I'm
concerned I'm the first real lover you've known. The
forced taking of a body doesn't count as love.'

'You're right, Bart, I know you are. But——'

'No "buts", Eve,' he said firmly. 'I love you, I'm going to marry you, and you're going to be the mother of my children. Nothing else matters,' he kissed her lingeringly. 'Nothing,' he repeated softly.

She knew that, and yet there was still a nagging doubt in her mind. Did Bart really believe her when she told him about Carl? Or would he one day turn around and accuse her of enjoying being Carl's mistress?

CHAPTER TEN

Eve was down in the kitchen with Maisie when Bart came down from his nap, fresh and alert, his eyes twinkling mischievously as he bent to kiss her on the mouth.

He sat down beside them on the breakfast stools, helping himself to some of the peas they were shelling. 'Have the two of you decided yet when Eve is going to make an honest man of me?' he enquired casually.

Eve gasped, blushing fiery red. She had felt shy about facing him again after the passion they had shared, and he came out with something like that!

It was Maisie who answered him. 'Behave yourself,' she chided. 'And leave those peas alone!' She slapped his hand as he went to take some more.

Bart put his arm about Eve's shoulders, grinning at her. 'Haven't you told Maisie yet about your having to marry me?'

'I——'

'Stop it, Bart,' the housekeeper told him firmly. 'You're embarrassing the poor girl.'

He looked down at Eve with wide innocent eyes. 'Am I embarrassing you, darling?'

'You know you are!'

He chuckled his enjoyment of the situation. 'I just love to see you blush. Seriously, when is the wedding?'

'I haven't told Maisie there was going to be one,' she told him shyly.

He looked up at the housekeeper. 'But I'm sure she guessed.'

'Of course I did,' Maisie confirmed scoffingly.

'Otherwise I would want to know the reason why.'

'You see,' said Bart in a stage whisper. 'I told you you'd have to marry me. You—Saved by the bell,' he grinned as the telephone began ringing out in the hallway. 'I'll get it, Maisie.' He stood up.

Eve didn't know where to look once she was alone with Maisie. How could Bart say such things!

'He always was incorrigible,' Maisie tutted. 'Even as a child.'

Eve's expression softened. 'He was?'

'Terrible. His poor mother was always apologising for his outspokenness.'

And she was going to have children exactly like that one day. Pleasure shot through her just at the thought of it, the love still shining in her eyes when Bart returned, her breath catching in her throat at how attractive he looked in the black silk shirt and fitted black trousers.

'I hope that look is for me,' he murmured throatily, bending to kiss her lingeringly on the mouth.

'Get out of my kitchen if you're going to carry on like that,' Maisie ordered firmly.

'Come on,' Bart chuckled to Eve. 'I'll take you into the lounge where I can ravish you in private.'

She went with him willingly. 'Maisie said you were incorrigible,' she told him crossly, 'and you are!'

He pulled her into his arms, his hands linked loosely at the base of her spine. 'I thought you already knew that.' He teased her lips apart, the light caress instantly taking on a more serious vein. He finally moved back with a sigh of satisfaction. 'When I woke up I thought I must have dreamt you.'

'I wouldn't have liked that.' Her arms were up about his neck, her body arched against his.

'Neither would I,' he rested his forehead on hers. 'I love you.'

'I love you too.'

'Sure?'

'Very sure. I—You aren't going away again, are you?' she asked worriedly.

'What——? Oh, you mean the telephone call. No, I'm not going away. It was my sister calling from New York.' He grimaced. 'She's coming over with her husband this week——'

'Oh yes, I forgot to tell you! Derek called, he said he and your brother-in-law were flying over.'

'My sister's coming with them. She's six months pregnant and yet she can't let David out of her sight.' He shook his head. 'They're so much in love they can't go a day without seeing each other. I feel the same way about you, darling,' he said at her hurt look. 'But when you're six months pregnant I intend staying at home with you, not flying off and leaving you.'

'And when you go away now?'

'You'll be with me,' he told her fiercely. 'I've reserved all your days and nights for the rest of our lives, and I don't intend losing a single one of them.'

She flushed her pleasure. 'Will your sister be here for the wedding?'

Bart grimaced. 'I'm under strict instructions for it to be Friday. Is that okay with you?'

'I wish it were sooner, but——'

'So do I!' he groaned. 'So do I, my darling. But you don't know my sister, she's likely to throw a fit if she can't see her one and only brother married off.'

Eve could understand that. It sounded as if the two of them were very close, despite Bart's mocking attitude.

'Friday will be fine,' she agreed. 'There's quite a lot to organise, anyway.' She played with the buttons on his shirt, slipping her hand inside when one of them accidentally came open.

'We can have a small reception here, I'm sure Maisie will love to do that for us. Stop that!' he shuddered as her hand caressed the downward path of the silky hair on his chest and navel. 'Eve, behave yourself!'

'But I like touching you!' she pouted.

'After Friday you can touch me all you want, in fact I shall insist on it.' He took her hand out of his shirt, rebuttoning it. 'But until then you settle for kisses.'

'Just—kisses?'

He laughed huskily. 'You're turning into a wanton! And there'll be no more sharing of my bed until we're married.'

She knew a deep disappointment. 'But I've been sleeping in that bed while you're away.'

'And tonight you can move back into your own room.'

'But, Bart——'

'Eve, what happened this morning was—beautiful, fantastic, everything I've ever imagined it would be like with you.' He kissed her lovingly. 'But it won't be repeated until we're married. This morning I let my desire overrule my judgment—mainly because I wanted you so damned much. I still do. But we have to be sensible——'

'Sensible!' she scoffed. 'I don't want——'

'Neither do I,' he groaned. 'But we have other people to think of besides ourselves. Maisie has probably guessed what happened——'

'Because you more or less told her!'

He smiled. 'I couldn't resist it. You blush so delightfully. As I said, Maisie knows I made love to you this morning, but she wouldn't approve of you moving into my room until I have my ring firmly on your finger.'

Eve felt her earlier foreboding come back to her. 'Are you sure it isn't just that you don't want me?'

'Not want you?' His fingers dug painfully into her arms. 'Of course I want you, don't be so damned stupid!'

She pulled away from him. 'I'm not being stupid! You——'

'Are we having our first engaged-couple argument?' Bart attempted to tease her.

But she wasn't in a mood to be teased; this shared love was all too new to her, her uncertainties were still too numerous. 'We aren't engaged!' she snapped. 'If you don't want to marry me, Bart, don't feel that you have to just because of this morning. *I* seduced *you*, remember?' she said bitterly.

His face darkened. 'Like hell you did!' he rasped. 'I wanted it to happen, I wanted *you*. And as for our not being engaged . . .' He dragged her into his study, deftly opening the wall-safe behind the watercolour that hung on the pale green wall. He took out a small black velvet box and flicked it open.

Eve gasped as the huge diamond winked and flickered in the sunlight, the size of it almost dazzling her. She had never seen such a ring; the delicacy of the gold band looked almost too slight to hold the weight of the diamond.

Bart roughly grasped her left hand and slid the ring on her third finger. It was slightly loose, but not enough to worry about. 'You've lost weight since I chose this for you,' he said gruffly, bending down to kiss her palm.

Eve shivered at the intimacy of the caress. Bart's eyes were a luminous green. 'You chose this for me?' she said huskily; the cost of such a ring frightened her.

He nodded. 'The same time as I chose the wedding ring,' and he showed her a second box in the wall-safe. 'But when——'

'The same time as I had the bed delivered.'

Her eyes widened. 'You were very sure of yourself!'

'I wasn't sure at all. I bought the bed and the rings to try and give myself hope. I saw you a lot of times before I actually spoke to you at the theatre. You were fantastic on stage, but off stage you were so cool, so removed from everyone. You frightened the hell out of me with your coldness. And that first night we met you were so contemptuous of me. It wasn't at all the way I had envisaged us being together. You didn't even like me, I could tell that, and——'

'It wasn't you I didn't like, it was the type.'

His face darkened to anger. 'I'm not a *type*, damn you! I'm me, Bart Jordan, and I can fall in love as easily as the next man. I'd loved you for months before I even got to speak to you. I was sure you must feel the same way when we met. But you didn't, you hated me, accused me of wanting to set you up as my mistress.'

'That was because——' she broke off, biting her lip to stop it trembling.

'Because . . .?' he prompted.

'After—after—You see, he said——'

'Tell me!' Bart ordered grimly.

She looked away. 'Carl was very like you, rich, handsome, very sure of himself.' She shivered as once again she remembered the gullible way she had been fooled by him. 'After I moved into the apartment he made it perfectly clear what I was there for. When I said I thought he had wanted to—to marry me, he told me that—that men like him didn't marry girls like me.' She looked up as she heard Bart draw in an angry breath. 'I thought you were the same, wanted the same thing from me.'

'And I was so damned angry I fell into the trap of letting you think that,' he rasped. 'That's why you didn't respond when I kissed you, isn't it?'

She nodded. 'All I could think of was that Carl had kissed me the same way.'

Bart took a step towards her. 'There was one fundamental difference,' he told her softly. 'I loved you.'

'He said he did too.'

'Oh, God!' he turned away with a groan. 'Am I going to lose you because of the actions of a man I don't even know?' He looked at her with tears shimmering in his eyes. 'If you leave me, Eve, I swear I'll——'

'Hush, darling!' She put her fingertips gently over his lips, her arms about his waist as she rested her head on his chest, the fast rate of his heartbeat telling her how upset he was. 'I'm not going to leave you,' she assured him, finally knowing that Bart loved her as much if not more than she loved him.

His face was buried in her throat as he trembled against her. 'You'll marry me?' he said gruffly.

She touched his hair lovingly. 'If that's what you want.'

'Oh God, yes!' His arms tightened painfully about her.

'Then we'd better start making the arrangements,' she said briskly, anxious to dispel the mood of despair she had unwittingly caused in Bart. 'I shall have to get something to wear, and——'

'White,' he looked up to say. 'I want you in white.'

She blushed. 'I thought perhaps something in cream or pale pink——'

'White,' Bart repeated firmly. 'It has to be white.'

'But——'

He looked down at her warningly. 'Do I have to choose it for you?'

He would too, she knew that. 'I'll wear white,' she agreed shyly. 'Although——'

His lips on hers stopped further conversation, and it

was a long time before either of them spoke again.

'I wish my aunt and uncle could be here for the wedding,' she sighed, held firmly in Bart's arms as they sat together on the sofa in his study.

Bart looked a little sheepish. 'They will be,' he revealed reluctantly.

'They will?' she cried excitedly, then suddenly frowned. 'But how?'

'After speaking to you on the telephone the other day I—um—I telephoned your uncle and told him we were getting married.'

'You did?' Her eyes were wide with disbelief.

'Arrogant of me, wasn't it?' he saved her the trouble of the accusation. 'But I thought that was what you had meant.'

She giggled. 'You would have looked very silly if I'd said no.'

'I wouldn't have let you. Oh, you might have said no to start with, but I would have just kept asking until you gave in. Judy's coming over with Derek, by the way. I asked my sister to arrange that.'

Eve gave him an exasperated look. 'There doesn't seem to be much to organise, you've done it all.'

'You can organise your things over to my room,' he grinned. 'And we'll go into town this week and buy you a new summer wardrobe, for your trousseau. Not that I expect you to wear much on our honeymoon, but you'd better take them just in case.'

'Just in case of what?' she teased.

He shrugged. 'We could have unwanted visitors. And only one nightdress, just in case of fire. I believe you know what your usual night attire is going to be?' he mocked.

Eve blushed as she remembered that conversation. 'You,' she recalled huskily.

'Exactly,' he said with satisfaction. 'Eve,' he

suddenly sobered, 'there'll be no more scares like just now? You'll marry me?'

'Yes,' but her voice lacked conviction.

'Eve?' he demanded strongly, shaking her gently. 'Promise me that no matter what doubts or fears you have you'll come to me with them, that you won't do anything without talking to me first? Promise me, Eve!'

'I—I promise,' she whispered.

He shook her again. 'Again! Say it louder. I want to hear you say it again.'

She looked up, her eyes flashing. 'You're a bully, Bart Jordan!'

His mouth was grim. 'You'd better believe it. You'll never get away from me now I have you. Never.'

Over the next few days she learnt that she didn't want to get away from him. She saw Bart as she had never thought he could be, the kind, openly affectionate lover who didn't care who knew how much he loved her. After Carl's offhand treatment of her Bart's love made her feel cherished and cared for, as if he were interested in her least little thought, as if nothing she said or did could ever bore him.

Without even being aware of it she blossomed overnight, in love and loved in return, each waking moment spent either with Bart or planning their wedding and the lengthy honeymoon they were to have on the Greek island Bart had borrowed from a friend of his, and if her nights weren't actually spent with him they were spent dreaming about him.

She put back on some of the weight she had lost, her face lost its tense, drawn look, her violet eyes no longer haunted but glowing with love. And she and Bart only had to look at each other for an electric current of awareness to shoot between them, desire never far from the surface, although firmly controlled by Bart as he kept to his decision not to make love to her again until they were husband and wife.

'Thank God tonight I don't have to go to bed alone,' he said with a groan as they drove to the airport on Friday to pick up his sister and her husband.

'It was your choice,' she said unsympathetically, grinning as he scowled at her.

'You'll get your punishment tonight,' he threatened. 'We'll see who teases who then.'

She blushed. 'I can hardly wait!'

His hand came out to grasp hers. 'Neither can I.'

'Do you think your sister will like me?'

'She'll love you.' His hand squeezed hers before he returned it to the steering-wheel, driving the limousine himself as they were to pick up Derek and Judy as well as the other couple. 'But even if she doesn't,' he added hardly, 'it isn't going to make any difference to the way I feel about you, or the fact that we're going to be married this afternoon.'

'This afternoon I shall be Mrs Bartholomew Jordan,' she breathed huskily. 'Doesn't it sound wonderful?' Her eyes glowed.

Bart smiled indulgently at her childish pleasure. 'I don't know, I've always been *Mr* Bartholomew Jordan.'

'Oh yes.' Her face dropped with disappointment.

'Don't look like that,' he laughed huskily. 'Tonight you can tell me just how wonderful it is being my wife.'

She looked out of the window, her nose high in the air. 'I'm not sure I should tell you, your ego is big enough already.'

'Then pander to it,' he teased.

'I'll think about it,' she told him primly.

Heathrow was as noisy as usual, planes landing every few minutes, the terminals full of people arriving and others trying to depart, the latter not always easy at this busy airport.

Eve frowned as they waited for the others to come through Customs, their plane having arrived twenty minutes earlier. 'Are you sure this won't all be too much for your sister? You remember how tired Aunt Sophy was when they arrived yesterday, and she isn't pregnant.'

'No,' Bart grinned. 'But she is over sixty. Here they come now!' He strode forward, Eve's hand held firmly in his as he took her with him.

Derek and Judy appeared first, closely followed by another couple, a couple in their mid-thirties, the man tall and dark, the woman equally tall, but her hair was silky and blonde, her slender body showing the advanced state of her pregnancy. The woman turned from laughing up at her husband, and her beautiful face was instantly recognisable to Eve. The woman was Helen Prentiss, although the man at her side wasn't Carl. Bart walked straight over to the other woman, kissing her affectionately on the cheek.

Eve at once felt sick. This woman, the woman who knew so much about her past, was Bart's *sister*.

CHAPTER ELEVEN

Eve stared as if in a daze, a hundred thoughts buzzing through her mind at the same time, and none of them making any sense, all of them disjointed. Helen Prentiss was now Helen Halstead. Carl had said she had a powerful family, but he hadn't mentioned that her family consisted of Bart. And now Helen was going to expose her to Bart, to tell him that his ex-brother-in-law had been the other man in her life.

'Eve,' Bart pulled her to his side, 'this is my sister Helen and her husband David,' he introduced. 'This is Eve Meredith,' he told them proudly. 'My fiancée.'

'Only until this afternoon, you lucky devil.' David slapped him on the back, his accent distinctly American. 'It's a real pleasure to meet you, Eve,' and he kissed her soundly on the cheek.

At any other time Eve would probably have liked him. He was a lot like Bart to look at, tall and dark, very handsome, with a confidence that went with extreme wealth and success. But at this moment she was too tensed-up to appreciate his easy charm, just waiting for the moment when his wife told Bart about her.

Helen was looking at her now, her eyes no longer the dull, cold blue Eve remembered. This second marriage was obviously making her ecstatically happy. Why didn't she just tell everyone that they had met before? Why didn't she say *something*?

'Helen?' Bart prompted impatiently, obviously aware of his sister's lengthy silence too, frowning darkly at her.

Helen looked up at him. 'Sorry, Bart,' she said softly.

'I was just so overwhelmed by your choice of bride.'

Eve bit her bottom lip painfully to stop it trembling, closing her eyes as she waited for the words that would wreck the happiness she had found this last week.

'She's beautiful, Bart,' Helen continued. 'Too beautiful and sweet for a rake like you,' she teased. 'Welcome to the family, Eve,' and she hugged her, kissing her warmly on the cheek.

Eve blinked up at the other woman, too dazed to make any reply. Beautiful and sweet, Helen had called her. She searched the other woman's face as she turned to laughingly hug her brother. Didn't Helen *remember* her? It appeared not, by her spontaneous welcome. But she would one day; she had to.

She turned to welcome Derek and Judy, aware that her smile was fixed, her happiness hanging by a tenacious thread.

'I'm really happy for you,' Derek hugged her.

'Me too,' Judy added.

'Not as happy as I am.' Bart's arm came possessively about her shoulders.

Helen laughed. 'No one could be as happy as you are. I've never seen you like this before,' she added gently.

His arm tightened. 'I'd never met Eve before.'

'Love certainly agrees with you,' his brother-in-law told him. 'Shall we all get out of this crush? Helen, are you okay?'

She did look a little pale. 'I'm just tired,' she smiled. 'One of Maisie's delicious lunches, a little nap, and I'll be just fine.' She put a hand through the crook of her husband's arm. 'I wouldn't miss seeing Bart get married for anything. I always remember he claimed he would never get caught in that trap.' She wrinkled her nose teasingly at her brother. 'What do you say now, Bart?'

He had got them all safely out of the airport terminal and into the limousine by this time. 'Once I'd met Eve,' he turned to smile at her, 'I walked right inside and locked the door behind me.'

If Eve was quiet on the drive the other five passengers in the car made up for it, all seeming to talk at once. She was just glad to rest her head back against the leather upholstery and be ignored. What was she going to do? How could she marry Bart knowing that one day his sister might remember that she was the girl she had once tried to buy out of her husband's life?

By the time they reached Bart's house she had a headache that made her temples throb, almost blinding her. She had been wanting to cry for the last hour, had known that the wedding everyone had been happily discussing would never take place. She couldn't marry Bart, not knowing her happiness could be ripped from her at any time.

'Are you all right, darling?' Bart frowned as they entered the house. 'You're looking very pale.'

'Nerves,' she dismissed. 'I—I'll just go into the lounge and say hello to Aunt Sophy and Uncle George, and then I—I think I'll go and rest for a while.' She gave him a jerky smile. 'I haven't been sleeping too well lately.'

He squeezed her hand. 'By all means rest, my love. The rest of the—day is going to be tiring.'

She knew he meant to tease, and yet she couldn't meet his humour, hastily excusing herself to go and talk to her aunt and uncle. They had arrived back from Egypt the day before, and would be leaving for Norfolk straight after the wedding—the wedding that wasn't going to be.

By the time she finally reached her room her throat ached from the effort of holding back the tears. Once in her room they were allowed to flow freely, her despair so deep she couldn't seem to stop crying once she had started.

This morning she had been so happy, looking forward to spending the rest of her life with Bart, and now she had only long, endless years without him in front of her.

She didn't hear the light knock on the door, or know that Helen Halstead had entered the room, until the other woman sat down on the bed beside her.

Eve spun round, hastily rubbing the tears from her face. 'What do you want?' she demanded in a choked voice. 'I—I thought I might rest before the wedding,' she invented, feeling as if she would never rest again.

Helen's expression softened. 'You have nothing to fear from me, Eve,' she told her gently.

Eve sat up, licking the tears from her top lip. 'I—I don't know what you mean.' She gave a bright meaningless smile. 'Shouldn't you be resting too?'

'I will be, in a moment. I wanted to come and talk to you first.' Helen stood up to pace the room, the deep blue maternity dress the colour of her eyes. 'I'll admit that when I first knew Bart was to marry you it was a bit of a shock to me.'

She knew! This woman already remembered exactly who she was. 'You didn't act shocked——'

'Not at the airport, Eve. I'm not talking about there. Bart told me over the telephone who he was marrying. I've never forgotten you——'

'I don't suppose you have,' Eve choked bitterly.

Helen shook her head. 'Not for the reason you mean. I've never forgotten what Carl did to you.' Her mouth twisted. 'I'd always known he was cruel, but what he did to you——! That I could never forgive. And he thought a few roses could make up for doing *that*,' she added with disgust.

Eve was deathly white. 'You—you know about——'

'Oh yes,' Helen gave a harsh laugh. 'Carl boasted of it to me. When I met you at the apartment I could see how upset you were, how shocked, and you were covered in bruises. When I asked Carl about it he thought it very amusing to tell me exactly what he'd done to you.'

'Oh no!' Eve buried her face in her hands.

Helen gently touched her arm. 'I told you he was cruel. He thought it would bother me. It did, but not in the way he expected. That day I took the children and left him. For years I'd put up with his behaviour, the humiliation of his other women, the way he used to get drunk and—Well, he was just an obnoxious human being. And knowing what he'd done to you gave me the courage to leave him. I felt so sorry for you, wanted to help you, but when I got back to the apartment you'd already gone. When Bart told me he was marrying someone called Eve Meredith I could hardly believe the coincidence. His description of you more or less confirmed my belief that you were the same Eve Meredith.'

'I'm sorry. I—I had no idea that you and Bart—— I can't marry him now.'

'Why can't you?' Helen demanded to know. 'He loves you——'

'Now,' Eve nodded. 'But not when he knows. Oh, he knows there was someone else, but not—but not——'

Helen's gaze was probing. 'You don't intend marrying Bart, do you?'

She shook her head. 'I can't.' She looked up with tear-wet eyes. 'I love him, but I can't marry him.'

'You can,' Helen said firmly. 'He loves you so much. I've never seen Bart so happy. He's completely different—carefree, boyish, and so proud of you.' She gave a tearful smile. 'I never thought I'd see my brother like that.'

Eve drew in a ragged breath. 'Will you help him when I—when I've gone? He won't understand, and— Tell him the truth for me.' She shivered. 'I couldn't bear for him to come after me and then have to let him go again.'

'You're making a mistake, Eve. Bart isn't like that.'

'Carl was his *brother-in-law*!' Eve cried.

'Yes,' Helen agreed heavily. 'All right, Eve, have it your own way. And I'll explain to Bart. I'll do that for you at least. I just wish——'

'Thank you, Helen,' Eve said shakily. 'I'd like to pack now.'

That wasn't so easy when she was crying as if her heart would break. And it felt as if it had. When Bart came bursting into the room she almost fainted, the room seeming to sway dizzily for several seconds.

'Eve!' His arms came protectively about her, holding her firmly against him. 'Oh God, Eve!' he groaned into her throat. 'You aren't leaving me. You can't!'

'Helen——'

'Yes, she told me.'

'She shouldn't have told you yet. When I'd gone——'

'I'd have throttled her if she'd waited until then. And she knew it. I know it all, Eve, and none of it makes the slightest bit of difference to the way I love you. If Carl were alive——'

'He's dead?' she gasped.

Bart nodded. 'About a year ago, in a road accident. He died the way he lived, violently. I had no idea of the life Helen led with him until she left him. Helen had always been too proud to let anyone know what a disaster her marriage to him was. God, now I know why you hated my roses,' he groaned. 'I sent red roses because to me they've always meant love, true love. To you they meant a reminder of the violence Carl showed you. When you're my wife——'

'You can't still want to marry me,' she protested.

'I'm *going* to marry you.'

'No——'

'Yes! And maybe in about fifty years I'll be able to give you red roses to show how much I love you.'

Tears filled her eyes, tears of happiness this time. 'I'll never destroy red roses from you again,' she choked. 'Oh, Bart, I love you!' She flung her arms about his neck, hugging him to her.

'I love you too. Just remember that, and the promise you made me, the next time you get the crazy idea of leaving me. I'd follow you, Eve,' he added deeply, 'and I'd find you, wherever you were. We have something special, darling, something that will never be destroyed. Do you believe me?'

'Yes,' she breathed huskily. 'Oh yes!'

And when she took the single red rose Bart handed her before they went before the registrar to make their marriage vows she knew that she did believe. Bart had given her his heart, and he would never take it back.

We value your opinion. . .

You can help us make our books even better by completing and mailing this questionnaire. Please check [✓] the appropriate boxes.

1. Compared to romance series by other publishers, do Harlequin novels have any additional features that make them more attractive?

   1.1 ☐ yes   .2 ☐ no   .3 ☐ don't know

   If yes, what additional features? _____

   _____

   _____

2. How much do these additional features influence your purchasing of Harlequin novels?

   2.1 ☐ a great deal   .2 ☐ somewhat   .3 ☐ not at all   .4 ☐ not sure

3. Are there any other additional features you would like to include?

   _____

   _____

   _____

4. Where did you obtain this book?

   4.1 ☐ bookstore   .4 ☐ borrowed or traded

   .2 ☐ supermarket   .5 ☐ subscription

   .3 ☐ other store   .6 ☐ other (please specify)_____

5. How long have you been reading Harlequin novels?

   5.1 ☐ less than 3 months   .4 ☐ 1-3 years

   .2 ☐ 3-6 months   .5 ☐ more than 3 years

   .3 ☐ 7-11 months   .6 ☐ don't remember

6. Please indicate your age group.

   6.1 ☐ younger than 18   .3 ☐ 25-34   .5 ☐ 50 or older

   .2 ☐ 18-24   .4 ☐ 35-49

Please mail to: **Harlequin Reader Service**

In U.S.A.	In Canada
1440 South Priest Drive	649 Ontario Street
Tempe, AZ 85281	Stratford, Ontario N5A 6W2

Thank you very much for your cooperation.

There is nothing like...

Harlequin Romances

The original romance novels!
Best-sellers for more than 30 years!